La Fem.

Also by
MADELEINE BOURDOUXHE

Marie
Sous le Pont Mirabeau
A Nail, a Rose

La Femme de Gilles

MADELEINE BOURDOUXHE

Translated and with an afterword by

FAITH EVANS

DAUNT BOOKS

This edition first published in 2014 by
Daunt Books
83 Marylebone High Street
London W1U 4QW

3

First published in 1937 by Gallimard, Paris
First published in Great Britain in 1992 by Lime Tree,
a division of Reed Consumer Books

A CIP catalogue record for this title is available
from the British Library

ISBN 978 1 907970 5 35

Typeset by Antony Gray
Printed and bound by TJ International
www.dauntbooks.co.uk

1

'Five o'clock,' says Elisa to herself. 'Soon he'll be home.' The thought paralyses her completely. She's spent the whole day polishing, washing, scrubbing, making a thick soup for supper – most people round here don't eat a proper meal in the evenings but Gilles works at the factory, and has only an egg sandwich for lunch. Now she finds herself transfixed, unable even to lay the table. Her arms hang helplessly, hopelessly, at her side. Giddy with tenderness, she clings to the metal rail of the stove, stock still, panting for breath.

This always happens a few minutes before Gilles gets back. Overcome by the thought of his return her body, drowning in sweetness, melting with languor, loses all its strength. She imagines rushing towards him, clasping him in her arms – but whenever she sees him actually appear in the doorway, sees the big muscular body and the corduroy work-clothes, she feels weaker still.

To Gilles, she always looks immobile, a bit distraught, and it's he who goes up to her and kisses her lightly on the forehead.

'Did you see the children?' she asks him. 'They went out to meet you . . . '

He pulls off his jacket and sits down, running his rough hands through his hair. His half-open shirt exposes the nakedness beneath, and Elisa watches as he gently scratches at the little tuft of hair on his chest. 'No, they've gone to play in the meadow with the others,' he replies. 'Why is it that kids always like other people's gardens better than their own – there's nothing wrong with our patch.'

'I'm not worried, just that it's time for their Saturday bath – I've got the big tub all ready, the water's warming in the sun.'

Now Elisa moves closer, inhaling from his clothes the strong mixture of sweat, iron, oil and work that clings to him and makes up his own masculine smell. Tenderly she rubs her face against his unshaven skin, caresses his ruddy cheek, his hair, his mouth, his eyes. 'Gilles . . . ' she says. When she speaks his name, it comes out as brief and wet as a whisper: saliva fills her mouth, moistening her curved lips and escaping at the corners in two tiny bubbles.

She goes back to the stove and lifts the cover of the pan a fraction, to release the smell of the soup. Gilles sniffs the air with all the greed of a starving man and, thinking of the treat to come, sighs deeply and longingly. She laughs.

'It's not nearly suppertime yet!' she says. 'Still, wait a moment . . . '

Handing him some rice pudding, she watches as he

gulps it down in three mouthfuls, then wipes his mouth in a grand gesture and pours himself a cup of coffee from the stove. His rough worker's trousers stay up on his strong hips without a belt; he has the same tall, lean, tough body as most of the workers in the area, but his beautiful eyes make him different.

Out in the garden Elisa leans her heavy, handsome body over the tub. To test the water she plunges in her bare arms, staying still for a moment, soaking in the softness. She looks at the reflection of her face; it is blurred by the shimmering sun, but by moving her head a little further down she reaches an area of shade in which her image is clearer: the long, full face, the regular features, the dark, shining hair. For a woman of the north, she has a strangely Spanish look about her.

Standing up, she runs her wet hands round her mouth, calls to the children and smiles back at Gilles, who is watching from the window. He loves this long, narrow strip of earth. Every Sunday in spring he dug and planted it himself; he built the redbrick dovecote, set the hedge of blackcurrant bushes and constructed the border of rocks by the stream that runs through the garden.

When they first saw the house he was in two minds about renting it; but then Elisa spotted the little stream. In those days she still had the body of a young girl, and Gilles watched her running towards the water, her small firm breasts bobbing up and down beneath her blouse.

The sight filled him with such a sense of happiness that he made up his mind on the spot.

Now he also liked the house, two rooms on the ground floor, two bedrooms above, and a big attic under the roof, with low windows.

Hearing the children arrive – two little blond twins, shy and well-behaved – Gilles goes back to the kitchen and takes one on each knee, breathing on their eyelids to make them laugh. He always feels moved when he sees both pairs of long eyelashes fluttering like this, and under his breath he murmurs: 'I'm so lucky – my two little girls.'

Elisa comes to collect the children for the bath and he again breathes in the smell of the soup, even more deeply this time. Supper will soon be on the table, and tomorrow is Sunday, so he won't have to go to work. Slowly his body begins to prepare itself for its long rest. When he wakes up, he will make love to Elisa. Sundays are best, because you have plenty of time ahead of you and you aren't drained by a hard day's work. There isn't much time for love-making on weekdays; though if he does manage it, it will still be in the morning, the weeks when he's on night shift at the factory. Walking home in the early-morning mist, Gilles will see the vigour of the day sprouting up all around him, and he will want to stake his claim on life before burying himself in the artificial night that for him follows the real one. On those mornings he hurries home, so as to find Elisa still in bed.

She is waiting for him, eyes tired from lack of sleep, because she sleeps badly when he isn't there. Sweetly, docilely, she lets herself be taken, fascinated by the expression of joy lighting up the face on top of her. And when Gilles, seized with a primitive, masculine pride, asks her awkwardly if she's enjoyed herself, she replies in all good faith; she cannot conceive of any greater happiness than giving him pleasure.

Afterwards she rises to prepare bread and butter and coffee so he can get to sleep as soon as possible. As she serves him she glances at him with a look of tenderness and shame: naturally modest, she is a little ashamed of making love so openly in broad daylight, in the pure, living sun of the morning, a little ashamed of feeling moved to such a pitch of tenderness.

He is leaning out of the window again, his mind at once blank and spinning with small thoughts: Sunday tomorrow . . . the smell of the soup . . . the beauty of the flowers in the garden. Life is sweet. As he watches Elisa bathing his two little naked daughters in the setting sun, he feels at peace.

2

Elisa had sat the children on the table to undress them for bed.

'Someone's come through the garden gate,' she said, looking out of the window. 'Oh, it's Victorine.

'You've turned up just in time to kiss the children good-night,' she said to the young girl who'd come in through the door. 'I was about to put them down. Won't you stay a few minutes? I won't be long.'

She took one of the little girls in her arms, pushed the other one in front of her and, breathing rather heavily, slowly climbed the spiral staircase that led up from the kitchen.

Gilles was quietly filling his big pigskin tobacco pouch.

'Nice day!' he said to Victorine.

'Sure,' she replied. 'It's all right here, because it's almost the country – but it's stifling in town, and it's just awful being shut up in a shop all day.'

Sitting at an angle to the table, facing Gilles, Victorine picked up a sheaf of trading stamps that Elisa left there and began mechanically sticking them into the book.

Desire takes hold suddenly, out of nowhere. Gilles saw

a little red mouth opening every few seconds to let the narrow tongue pass through, saw it licking a small square of paper lightly caressed by two fingers. He was dumbfounded, unable to move. He'd often felt spontaneous desire when looking at Elisa, a desire that surged up in him gently, pleasantly. This was different. This time his whole body was seized by a great wave of panic, and he thought his head would burst with blood.

He tried to think straight. 'She's Elisa's baby sister, for heaven's sake, I've known her for years, I can remember her with a plait on her back, and then a chignon . . . It's only little Torine, pull yourself together.'

It didn't work. As she went on sticking her stamps it was as though he was seeing those lips opening, that tongue darting in and out, for the first time in his life. He got up, walked round the table, leaned up against the oven rail and just stood there, his eyes enormous and staring at Victorine.

Pull yourself together, Gilles, no great harm has been done yet: it's not too serious, a great outburst of male desire, born spontaneously, thoughtlessly, deep in the flesh. The main thing is to pay it no attention – then it'll go away of its own accord, as illogically as it came.

But just then the little bitch raised her head. She was one of those women who know instantly, who never let an opportunity pass. Some people find it's their heart that develops immoderately as they grow up; for

Victorine it was always sex that took first place. There was nothing the poor child could do about it, she was born like that – which doesn't make it any less disgusting. She crossed her legs and, pretending to be tired, stretched luxuriously, with a funny, sweet little sigh.

Then, snatching another look at the expression on Gilles' face to check she'd got it right, she closed the book of stamps and went up to him. She looked at him: yes, he was a good-looking fellow, with his manly legs, his manly body, his manly shoulders . . . Victorine pressed her whole body against his.

Five seconds too late, Gilles realised that he was possessing the small red mouth, feasting on the faint taste of adhesive still on her lips. His legs shook and he couldn't move, even when they heard Elisa coming down the stairs.

Victorine slipped deftly back into her chair and began to hum a popular song, her fingers drumming on the table.

'They took a long time to go down,' Elisa said. She leaned towards the coal scuttle, intending to pull it towards her – Gilles' feet were in the way and she waited for him to move, her hand outstretched. Taking in every inch of his big, still figure – his legs, his torso, his shoulders – she smiled affectionately when she came to his dazed face, his vacant eyes.

'What's the matter with you? Move out of it, you silly ass!' Laughing, she placed a big noisy kiss on his cheek. He was her whole world.

'Would you like to eat with us?' she asked Victorine.

'All right,' the young girl replied, getting up to help her lay the table.

Gilles ate his soup in silence while Victorine told a tale about the cashier in the shop where she worked. Elisa ate well; she hadn't a care in the world. Gilles helped himself to some potato and bacon fritters but left his plate half empty.

'Don't you like it? Shall I do some eggs?' Elisa asked.

'No, I'm not hungry, I don't feel too good.'

She looked at him, worried.

Gilles could feel Victorine's leg rubbing against his. There seemed to be no air at all coming through the big window, wide open to the night. He thought he would die of heat; he longed for one of the women to leave the room.

Later, when Victorine had gone, he looked around him again, at the table, the chairs, the clock, the calendar, and thought, 'Everything is just the same as it always was.' He could not face up to what was happening to him.

For some minutes he said nothing; it was the first time he'd ever noticed the way objects and atmospheres change according to noise or silence. He then began to find the silence intolerable, heavy as lead.

'I'm going to take a look at the pigeons,' he said abruptly.

'At this hour?' asked Elisa. It was unusual for him to go out so late. 'All right, if you want to, but you'll wake them up . . . '

Outside, he went past the dovecote, turned right at the side of the house, climbed the concrete steps to the gate and bent over it. A white blouse would stand out in the dark; but no, there was no one on the road. His eyes scanned the darkness right to the bottom of the garden. Then, slowly descending the steps, he leaned against the wall of the house and murmured: 'What's happening to me?'

He pushed open the door of the dovecote. He loved the smell of grain and feathers, but this evening he didn't inhale it wholeheartedly, as he usually did. Mechanically he lit a match, looked, saw nothing.

'Are you coming in, my beloved, shall we go to bed?' called Elisa from the door of the house.

He went back into the house and pulled the little chain on the gaslamp, then felt his way towards Elisa, who was waiting for him at the foot of the stairs. They went up as they always did, Elisa walking slightly sideways, one arm flung around his shoulders.

3

'I'm sure there's nothing wrong – it's me who's changed, not him – he does the shopping as usual, goes to union meetings, takes the coffee over to Mother – it's me, it's my condition.'

Elisa was on the fourth concrete step. She scraped the snow off this one just as she had the others, throwing it into a little heap on the left, and swept until the concrete was clear. Then she knelt down on the clean step ready to attack the fifth. 'There, just a tiny bit higher . . . '

Straining hard she plunged her left hand into the snow and saw the imprint of Gilles' studded shoe. The muscles of her face tensed, as if she were short of breath. 'Dear little heart . . . ' She had not pronounced the words, but her lips quivered to their rhythm.

Up one more step, and there, the most satisfying task of all – a great slab of snow to push off all in one go. She brushed the step clear, moved on to another heap: 'All these little heaps . . . I'll ask Gilles to shovel them up with the spade. The trouble is, as soon as I ask him to do it I know he'll get that new expression on his face . . . '

She turned round, sat down on a step still covered in

snow, and stayed there for a moment, brush in hand. She could picture Gilles so clearly, sitting in front of the fire, legs stretched out, feet resting on the door of the open stove, with that new look of drowsy satiation. His head would move forward and backward in little jerky movements as if drawn by a will that was only semi-conscious; then he'd pull himself up abruptly, sharply, as though he'd been snorting, his attractive face looking somehow crumpled, the veins on his forehead standing out. If she said to him, 'Would you mind clearing up the snow with the spade?' he'd answer, 'I don't give a damn about those heaps of snow,' and that new look would come over him. He'd sit down and make himself comfortable, sniffing, spitting noisily into his handkerchief, smiling greedily, fixedly, into the stove. Those heaps of snow, what a lot of fuss about nothing.

'No, it's me,' she said to herself, 'Everything seems funny to me at the moment, it's my condition. Was I like this with the twins? Ouch! Another little kick, right in the middle of his mother's belly: he's going to be a strong one, all right. Oh yes, it must be me, surely. I ought to just get on with it.'

She attacked the next-to-last step.

Then she descended gingerly, keeping close to the wall, so as not to slip, in her over-large clogs. When she came to the door of the house she took them off and, holding them in her hands, walked silently in on her wet-stockinged feet, her eyes fixed on her swollen belly. Proudly she carried forward the new weight which had come to her from Gilles' body.

Today he was a little late coming in, and he had Victorine with him.

'I've brought the kid with me,' he said. 'She seemed bored at home, and since you go out so rarely now, I thought I might take her for a walk later.'

'Good idea,' Elisa said.

She looked proudly at her little sister, so pretty and so fresh; thinking of her own increasingly heavy and misshapen body, she said to herself, 'I'm glad he's going to take her out, it'll make a change for him.'

She was ashamed to have felt that vague sense of unease in the afternoon, and to reassure herself she asked him, 'Would you like to shovel up the heaps of snow with the spade? I've left them on the steps.'

'Sure,' he said, 'I'll do it right away.'

She looked at him with a big, happy smile.

Whistling, Gilles went out and slid the spade under the first heap, thinking to himself, 'Can't see any reason not to clear up the snow if that's what she wants – means damn all to me.'

Elisa had served supper early so they could get off.

'I don't have much money on me,' Gilles said as they were leaving.

'I'll give you some,' Elisa said. 'Where are you going, anyway?'

'Not sure – the cinema probably.'

Victorine, in gloves and hat, was all ready to go, leaning on the table with both hands. He was very close to her.

Turning her back on the room, Elisa stood by the wardrobe and rummaged in her handbag. Money in hand, she was about to snap it shut when, at precisely that moment, anxiety again took hold of her. It was no longer a vague feeling of unease that disappeared almost as soon as she had abandoned herself to it; this time the anguish was heavier, more acute. One by one she fixed her gaze on some of the objects around her, the things that made up her familiar world, then her eyes lit on her own hands as they closed the bag, and she saw they were trembling. Precisely at that moment Elisa knew that behind her back there was another world, a world that was complicated, threatening, unknown. She felt it to be so and she was certain she was not mistaken; she was also certain that it was absolutely essential not to turn round suddenly and confront it.

Disturbed by this mysterious insight, which seemed suddenly to have seized her by the throat, she waited a moment before slowly turning, at first only halfway, looking straight in front of her with faraway eyes, then three-quarters, then at last full face. She looked at them both. They seemed not to have moved: they were in exactly the same position they had been in a few minutes earlier, before she had had her insight.

Elisa walked up to them quite normally and gave Gilles the money, as though nothing had happened. She knew she was going to speak. She didn't know what she would say, but she knew it wouldn't be a sentence that dropped carelessly from her lips, but rather an essential sentence, a sentence of which she would be the perfect mistress.

Gilles put the money in his purse, picked up his hat.

'Shall we go?' he said, looking at Victorine.

Then Elisa said:

'I've been thinking – it's not tiring, going to the cinema . . . I think I'll come with you after all, I'll ask Marthe to look after the children. Wait for me a minute.'

She slipped on her coat and went to warn her neighbour, not stopping for a moment to see their astonished faces. When she got back all three walked down the slippery, muddy road in silence. The air was bitter, and Gilles pushed up his collar. Both women put one arm through his, their other hands keeping their furs tightly pressed against their mouths. They walked fast. In spite of the weight of her belly Elisa had no difficulty in placing her feet steadily on the stones of the road, and she let her eyes range brightly over the houses as they passed them, looking first right then left, keenly registering everything that came into her vision. She noticed every dirty little icicle that shone in the rivulets against the pavement; she marked the exact point at which the halo round the street-lamps disappeared into the sky. Passing in front of a lit window she saw a woman leaning over a half-cleared table; she had time to observe her face, her hair, her mouth, her gestures, her life. In that one look, which had lasted merely the few seconds that it takes three walking figures to cross a rectangle of light, Elisa came to know that woman. And she knew that the two people who walked beside her – at the same rhythm and on the same road, who saw as she did the icicles, the luminous fog of the street-lamps and the closed doors or lit windows that tinged women's lives with a sad light – they had no real knowledge of such things at all. Elisa felt a deep sense of pride, untouched by scorn, rising within her and comforting her soul.

They reached the stop and waited for the tram that would take them into town. No one had uttered a word.

Sitting in the dark cinema, Elisa had the vague sensation that she was now in her place: between Gilles and Victorine, in a shadowy unknown that was a part of the threatening world she had recently glimpsed. She didn't know why she felt this but it provided comfort and succour, released her from the need to delve or understand. She was still in that state of euphoria with which our hearts protect us in the midst of danger.

But later, when they had taken Victorine home and greeted her parents, when Elisa had gone to bed and heard Gilles' first snores, she felt she was breathing in a world that had returned to normal. Deprived of the feeling that she must act – for reasons both compelling and obscure – she gained the shattering liberty of looking things in the face. Now she could give careful thought to the disturbing sense of malaise that had weighed on her for several weeks; she could strip it right down until it delivered up its secret.

Searching her memory she peered slowly backward in time. Instead of articulating her thoughts she simply allowed the images to file past: Victorine, then Gilles, then Victorine again, then Gilles and Victorine. Sometimes, as if working faithfully and mechanically to a pre-arranged command, her memory would stop at a gesture, an attitude, or the end of a smile which, taken unawares by an unexpected glance, had lingered stupidly on. And again the images filed past, fast and irrelevant or heavy, confidential and suddenly arrested, to be submitted to the close scrutiny of the investigator. Victorine, Gilles and Victorine . . . And always there would come into her mind, like a leitmotif, that new face of Gilles', the face upon which Elisa's anxious eyes, searching for the familiar, had recently seen cruel, illegible signs.

From every image there came a new fragment of information, a painful little abstraction. None of these fragments was expressed in words, they were silent and without obvious meaning, but they accumulated in her heart and from this mysterious collaboration there would emerge a simple grammatical proposition to sweep away all the irrelevant images to come. In time, all the fragments would be reassembled in a precise truth – astonishingly short, and wholly contained in a fierce little group of words.

Elisa herself now put a halt to the march-past of images. She thought: 'For several weeks something has been going on between Gilles and Victorine. It may even be too late to prevent the worst.'

But these were only stages in the process. She waited a moment, gathering her forces, and then deliberately, courageously, stuck the knife into her own heart: 'Gilles no longer loves me.' Then she wavered, stretching her arms out to the sleeping man in a large, clumsy movement as if asking him for help, but stopped herself just in time. No, Elisa, this time you will have to suffer alone. For the first time in your life you cannot draw on Gilles' love, you must stand up for yourself as if you were quite alone in the world. No one can help you, least of all Gilles. You are alone with the greatest pain you have ever known.

Waves of grief, each one stronger than the last, began to engulf her. Afraid that she would give way, risking everything, she suddenly threw back the blankets and slipped out of bed. Gilles stirred and said in a sleepy voice: 'What's the matter?'

She managed to say, 'I'm dying of thirst . . . I'm going down to get a glass of water.'

She left the room with teeth clenched and arms outstretched, groping her way in the dark. Closing the kitchen door behind her she fell to her knees by the dead stove. Every few seconds, with the impact of each sob, her head rose, fell back, then down again into her arms, which lay still on the freezing metal.

By the time she returned to the bedroom her body was exhausted, her head swollen and painful, the arch of her brows setting off a fierce throb. Somehow, back in bed, she found the strength to stretch right out, as close as possible to the edge: her tears hadn't finished, and if her hand or her leg came anywhere near Gilles' familiar warmth she knew that a huge sob would engulf her and she'd leap up, yelling and shaking him by the shoulders, violently defying him not to love her. But all he would see in the feeble glow of the night-light would be a dishevelled woman leaning over him, swollen-faced, a pathetic flannel nightgown covering her misshapen body; a woman whose deep, blundering pain was her only means of trying to keep him. And she could feel tears welling up again, taste them on her lips and hands. Everything now was impregnated with tears – her hair, her face, her arms, her nightdress.

The smell of suffering always disgusts others, she thought. I must keep still, arms tightly at my side. She stopped moving.

But the tears started again without her knowing it: they flowed, of their own accord, all the way down her cheeks, hot at first, then slipping cold into her neck. Transfixed by a slack grief that repressed thoughts or images, she had no idea whether she'd been lying there for minutes or for hours. Some of the time she didn't even know the cause of her misery. Although her tears were silent she felt she was suffocating: if she so much as blew her nose Gilles would wake. I must pull myself together, she thought, there is too much at stake. Wrinkling her fine forehead, she firmed her jaw and stared at the window.

Outside she could see whitish rays of light. It was only the artificial dawn of the snow-filled world – but thinking that night was nearly over, she began to panic, fearing that Gilles would soon be awake. She looked out anxiously for brighter rays of light, but nothing moved in the whiteness. She had the sense that she was receiving some mysterious help from outside; she blessed this friendly dawn, which seemed to last for ever.

Eyes wide open to a false hope, she tried to grieve without weeping.

4

The next morning Elisa got up as usual and prepared Gilles' coffee and bread and butter. Nothing in her manner betrayed her. Her eyes were still swollen, but these days it wasn't surprising she should sometimes wake up looking tired.

When he'd gone she started the day's work as normal, polishing the top of the stove and cleaning the kitchen tiles more thoroughly than ever. But sometimes she would stop dead in the middle of a task and remain stock still for a moment, eyes fixed. She wasn't examining the past again, or wondering what attitude to take: she was simply thinking through the discovery she'd made the night before. She knew she had to take action but she didn't want to hurry – first she needed to get used to the idea. Each time she would repeat the same thing, then go back to her housework, straining to find an outer equilibrium in a world of household objects, familiar gestures, daily tasks. The work still had to be done.

In the early evening she fed the children and got them ready for bed. This meant that Gilles could play with them as he liked to when he came home, but she could take them straight up the moment she sensed that he wanted to smoke his pipe, read the paper or just sit in silence.

The days passed, and every time she saw or did something for the first time since her discovery it was like a new trial that had to be overcome. Once, standing high up in the window of the attic and seeing the garden and stream from this particular perspective, the clutch of happy memories which suddenly exploded in her heart tortured her so cruelly that she nearly gave in to her panic; she wanted to dash back to the kitchen and fall at Gilles' feet, begging him to confess all the tiniest details to her, or to hurt him as badly as she'd been hurt, battering him with the fists she now held clenched against her cheeks, until he swore he'd never see Victorine again.

But after a few days, when she had succeeded in completing the cycle of her weekly work, the catastrophe gradually lost its acute, revelatory nature; her environment began to seem less alien, alarming, unreal. Having succeeded in imparting a reflection of her misfortune to the objects around her, they now matched the grief that impregnated her heart and her flesh, and regained their familiarity. Her monotonous existence, which had once run quite naturally on a course of happiness, now ran, just as naturally, on a course of misery.

In her wisdom she kept her secret sealed: no one knew about the change inside her, the pact she'd made with her heart and the objects around her. She still smiled her beautiful sincere smile, still moved with life and grace, her big dark eyes still shone and smiled upon others.

5

When Sunday came round again Elisa knew that she must lose no more time, she must think about the future. First of all she must find out what stage things had reached. Exactly what had taken place between them? When did they see each other, and where? Since she couldn't very well ask those questions, she'd have to watch them, check up on all their movements; she'd have to follow Gilles whenever he left the house without a quite specific end in view, such as going to the factory.

At about four o'clock he stretched noisily and said, 'I'm popping out for a bit.' His voice came through a yawn that suggested the boredom of a man dulled by sleep, so the sentence sounded quite natural.

Elisa had handed him his cap and his leather jacket.

'Don't be too late,' she'd said affectionately, kissing him.

But as soon as he'd shut the door behind him she threw her coat over her shoulders and said to the twins: 'Be good! I'll be back in a moment.'

It was already dusk, but she immediately picked out Gilles' tall shape ahead of her. Keeping to the darkest part of the road she walked as quietly as she could. She saw a man passing Gilles, coming towards her: it could easily be a friend or an acquaintance, so she began to run, to make him think that Gilles had left the house before her and that she was catching him up. But when the man passed by without greeting her she resumed her slower pace, always keeping the same distance between Gilles and herself.

At the baker's Gilles stopped and went in; she carried on walking, then stopped at the edge of the square of light flooding out on to the road, somewhat disconcerted. He seemed to have entered the shop in all innocence, and was chatting with a friend in the back room.

What next?

Near the right wing of the house she saw an empty garden, with little bowers of Virginia creeper, where on fine summer days coffee and cakes would be served to people who'd walked out from town. In winter there were neither tables nor chairs, only little wooden benches left behind in each arbour. Making a sudden decision to wait for a few moments, she walked into the first arbour and sat down on the damp wood. She wanted to slip into the sleeves of her coat but she was afraid of the cold which would instantly penetrate her naked arms; so she stayed there, her garment wound tightly round her like a blanket, a little dark mass, scarcely visible in the dark bower. The light from a feeble street-lamp filtered between the leafless vine-stems, projecting a very soft glow on to her cheek.

In the white snowy distance she could see, lightly veiled in mist, the sturdy outline of the factory where Gilles worked. The furnaces never went out – there were day, night and Sunday shifts – and they reddened the fog from all four corners of the building. She thought back to her childhood, when she had been fascinated by those gaping mouths that spat eternal fire.

As a little girl she would go with her mother to help her carry the linen she'd ironed to clients who lived on the outskirts of town. For Elisa the glowing furnaces were the chief attraction of these trips: as soon as they came into sight she would kneel on the bench in the tram and press her face against the misty window, staring out at the red and blue flames which rose high and strong amidst the shooting sparks.

She loved those little journeys that she made each week with her mother. When they returned to town they'd cross the centre by tram and walk through a dark, deserted area to get to the river; from there you could see a really long way, and at night you could distinguish the blurred outline of distant hills. In the evenings it was hard to tell the difference between the slopes that were gentle and covered with greenery and the black, treeless slag-heaps – until the moment when a mysterious spark of fire escaped down the side of one of the slopes, separating it from the others. Only seconds earlier they had seemed like sisters. An image from her schoolbook would leap into her mind, and she'd think: 'It's like a volcano.' She'd follow the little fiery descent as if in a trance, never letting her eyes stray from the spark for a moment, until it came to a halt, grew dimmer, and finally, gradually, disappeared for good.

Throughout this spectacle she would keep softly repeating to herself, in an undertone, as if it were a refrain too strange to be spoken: 'I'm in Italy, I'm in Italy . . .' So distracted was she that she'd even overlook the presence of her mother, and the squeaky wicker basket, full of dirty washing, that they carried between them. She'd let her arm fall, and since she was so much smaller than her mother, the full weight of the load of washing, which had dropped into the lowest point of the basket, would hit her bang on the calf. Her mother would cry out: 'Careful, Elisa, stand up straight, you're taking all the weight of the basket!'

She'd straighten up the basket then, holding her hand high on her hips so as to keep it level. She only did this to please her mother – keeping her arm folded back was more painful than the load resting on her straightened arm, more painful even than the wicker scratching her calf.

Once the two handles of the basket were back at the same level Elisa's mother, her conscience clear, would say no more, and the little legs, bare and red with cold, would resume their automatic course along the deserted wharves where every now and again a wide-bodied bridge, or the flat outline of a moored barge, would emerge through the icy fog. But Elisa's eyes were on the horizon, greedily searching for the lost hill which had so recently revealed its sparkling truth. At last she'd find it, high above the houses and the factory chimneys, shining little lights dotted all over its dull mass. She couldn't be quite sure it was the same one, because the hills had resumed their inscrutability. But she'd been so dazzled by the image of the volcano that merely by thinking again of that refrain, so silent and at the same time so strangely inadequate – 'I'm in Italy, I'm in Italy' – she could recapture a delicious sense of unease.

Leaving the dark quayside, they'd pass through narrow, faceless streets to the dingy light of the shopping area. Back to normal. Faced with everyday life, the refrain and the image of the would-be volcano would disappear, and once they reached home, where the smell of ironing and steaming-damp linen filled the air, she'd think no more of it. On top of the stove there was an oddly-shaped pot containing irons stacked in a circle: sitting next to it, she'd open a book and start her homework. Elbows on knees, hands on brow, she'd read through sentences that seemed quite meaningless but that she did her best to repeat and learn. Her eyes were on a flounce of linen, as it swirled out and rippled in the light steam, then fell elegantly back into place, its movements dictated by her mother's ironing.

With her sticky little hands Victorine would clutch at the piles of clean linen, irritably demanding her mother's attention.

'Oh, I wish she'd shut up! Can't you do something to amuse her?'

Elisa would then put Victorine on her knee and bounce her up and down to the rhythm of a fairground song – until the trot developed into a frenetic gallop and she briskly pushed her down, as joyless children do, unconsciously turning a younger sister into a plaything. Her mother would shout: 'Don't jolt her like that!'

Ashamed, Elisa would clasp little Victorine in her arms, kiss her, smooth the folds of her pinafore, adjust her hair. How many times, when holding her like this, had she persisted in her efforts to make her even prettier than she was by trying to fix a ribbon in her short, babyish hair.

As they unfolded in her heart, these trivial memories lent a sort of stupor to Elisa's pain. A sense of unease compounded her grief. In the light of the past, the present became shocking, disturbing: normal laws seemed no longer to operate; there was something unacceptable about it all. Elisa felt as though she were walking on quicksands. After all, Gilles had only gone out to chat with a friend . . .

What was she doing, she thought, sitting here all alone in the cold and dark? Momentarily blinded by hope, she wanted to get up and go back to her children: she blamed herself now for leaving them alone. But she didn't move. Looking around her at all the blurred shapes of the night, at the glimmers of light shrouded in fog, once more she felt an infinite sadness rise within her.

What did it matter if the children were left alone? She loved these two little blond girls, who had Gilles' hair and her eyes, loved them with all her body and soul, the only way she knew how to love, the way she loved the child inside her now, whose life she could feel beating against her heart.

Although Elisa may seem to be the perfect mother, the love she bears for her issue does not spring from a maternalism of the heart or flesh. Children, for her, are the natural extension of the love she feels for her man, issue of his flesh, occupants of his home, their full value contained only in the shining light of that love.

So is she a woman made entirely out of the flesh of a spouse, a woman destined for procreation and the hearth? As she sheltered in her little cradle of greenery, a small shadowy mass even darker than the shadows surrounding her, creature among creatures, made of the same troubled, painful flesh, Elisa felt apprehensive, numb with cold. Why should she have been created to find fulfilment only in this manner?

One day Elisa had walked into her father's narrow workshop, filled with the smell of fresh shavings, and had seen a tall, fair young man standing in the doorway, his arms full of freshly-planed rifle-butts. A fateful encounter.

'Thanks, Gilles!' her father said. 'Tell your papa you can come and fetch some more next week.'

Gilles had greeted the man and the young girl with his wide, touching smile.

Elisa pictured him now, in the back room of the baker's shop, behind the wall she was leaning on. How handsome he was! In spite of his size, and although he was so strongly built, he still seemed just as young as then, still had that gentle look about him. He'd be talking to his friends with that same melting, rather slack smile that seemed to spread all over his face. Sitting up straight now, Elisa smiled too, full of love and pride. This man was hers, she thought: she loved him so much that she had the right to fight for him, to keep him for herself, for herself alone. Nothing could change that, nobody else had the right – not even Gilles himself – to separate them. Whatever happened, whatever had already happened, the main thing was not to make a fuss, simply to watch, and act in subtle little ways to keep intact the love with which she'd surrounded him, and to which he would return one day. There was no escape from a love as strong as hers.

She stayed like this for a while, sitting up straight, arms clenched against her chest under the half-open coat, tense in her unshakeable pride. Then she saw the door of the shop opening, heard Gilles' voice saying goodbye as the door closed behind him, heard his footsteps continuing on their way.

She followed him again through the darkness, keeping several metres behind. As the houses began to thin out, Elisa held close to the long, black, snow-covered hedges. She passed a little café, silent and mysterious, its windows covered in steam. Before long, she thought, they'd come to the point where the road crossed open fields: why on earth would he want to go there? Perhaps he just needed the fresh air . . . He was walking so fast that she had trouble keeping up with him. She'd been in such a hurry to leave the house that she was still wearing her old shoes, so down-at-heel that she had to move in painful, jerky little steps. The snow was beginning to melt and she walked into an icy patch of mud, which went right through the leather and soaked her stockings.

Where was he going now, for heaven's sake? This was hardly the weather for a stroll in the country . . . Now there were fields on both sides; and ahead, though still far away, the lights of the neighbouring village. For one moment she turned her head to look at the great expanse of white to her right; and when she turned back she'd lost sight of him. Breaking into a run, she could no longer see anything at all – there were no street-lamps and she couldn't see a single house . . . she could make out a second road to her left, and another a little further up, but where had he gone? Suddenly she felt very alone, very cold and very tired. She had to sit down: on anything. There was a big heap of stones at the side of the road and she sat on them, longing to call out his name. But it was only a thought: all that came out was a barely audible whisper. Perhaps he'd stopped not far from here – perhaps he'd hear her, come and help her get up, and they'd go back down the road together, with him holding her gently by the arm. Back home in the comforting warmth of the evening they'd talk about this and that, and to warm themselves up they'd drink the coffee that she'd make as soon as they got in. Holding their hands round the mugs they'd let the heat rise gently up through their fingers.

How absurd she'd been to leave the house like that, without even putting warm clothes on – in her condition, too! And what had she achieved? Absolutely nothing. You might think all you have to do is follow someone for light to dawn, but she'd come no closer to finding out what was going on, and here she was all alone, sitting on a heap of stones – tired, perished, and burdened by love.

She must get back. Her shoes were still full of water, and as she walked she moved her big toes around in them to try and warm her feet, but it didn't help. She'd left the children alone: they might even be crying, calling out, afraid. How long since she'd left them – an hour, two hours, longer? Probably not: you lose all sense of time if you wait alone in an arbour, and the cold walk up the road had seemed interminable, but it really didn't take longer than half an hour to walk from the fields to the house. Time to move! How much does it count in the scheme of things, she thought, that I walked up that black, deserted road with cold feet, exhausted? Get on with it, it's hardly a matter of life and death. She sighed 'Oh, Gilles!' and this time she said it aloud, softly but clearly.

Elisa made her way back across the fields until she reached the lights of the first house on the road. She thought there was no one outside it – but then she spotted a man leaning against the wall of the house: she could see the tip of his cigarette. As she came up to him he held out his hand as if to clutch her as she went past – but on seeing her close to, he pulled back, whistling in surprise. 'Wow, you've been getting your share all right, I can see that!'

She didn't respond, and without slowing her pace gave him a big calm smile. The man went on watching her but she moved away with her regular, firm, now rather heavy step. Soon he lost sight of her, as she merged with the darkness.

Gilles was back at eight o'clock, his cheeks red with cold, his jacket sparkling with melted snow.

'What a night!' he said, shaking himself on the step.

'Quite a walk,' Elisa said. 'Where did you go?'

'First to the baker's for a few minutes, then into town, to see a bit of life . . . '

'Ah!' In her mind's eye she saw him coming out of the baker's and walking on, turning his back on the town.

'Take your shoes off, they're soaked.' Reaching behind the stove, she handed him his warm slippers. 'You got this wet in town?'

'No, just walking back up the road was enough,' he said.

'Of course . . . '

Gilles stretches his legs, wriggles his toes inside the warm slippers. 'It's so nice and warm here,' he says. 'Is supper on?'

'It's ready.'

When he'd finished eating he rummaged in his pocket and said, 'I've brought you something.' He handed her a packet of caramels.

'That's nice of you,' she said, in a slightly restrained voice, and got up to thank him with a kiss. She leaned against him, rather heavily, suddenly letting herself go.

He played with the material of her blouse as he did so often, then placed his hands under her beautiful breasts and gently lifted them towards him. Elisa laid her head on his shoulder and stayed still, surprised to feel so content.

It didn't help to understand what was going on. Here he was being as gentle and as loving as always, and he'd thought about her, bought her sweets – so why did he lie like that, telling her he'd gone into town? It was all so strange and impenetrable. Perhaps there was nothing wrong after all.

She was worn out. After walking back at speed she'd washed the children and put them to bed, then she'd carried out various little household tasks so that everything would be ready for Gilles' return. Now she'd have liked never to move or think again, just to stay here resting against him, kissing him every few moments with little wet kisses; she'd have liked to fall asleep with her mouth half-open on his neck. Gilles holding her breasts as she kissed him was such a familiar pose that it seemed to lock the present into the tenderness and security of the past, when every moment, every word had been a source of reassurance.

'Let's go to bed, Elisa my sweet.'

He moved his hands up to her shoulders and away from her whilst she disentangled her arms from his, breaking the spell. Then she rescued his shoes from their little puddle of water and put them to dry. They'd taken him out through the grey, icy mud, all through the snow-covered fields . . . Where had he stopped? What was that unknown destination? Was it Victorine? Victorine . . . Gilles and Victorine . . .

'Coming?'

'Coming . . . '

In bed he didn't turn round straight away but stayed leaning against her, murmuring those odd little phrases, harbingers of love, that she knew so well. Feeling his hands move down her body she recoiled ever so slightly.

'Are you afraid for the little one? It's not dangerous, you know . . . '

'Why didn't you make love to me this morning like you usually do?'

'How should I know?'

As he lay brusquely on top of her she thought she could see something like a glimmer of revenge in his eyes, possibly the burden of pent-up desire.

Beware of a blunder, let him come back to you whatever the reason, don't show false pride. No danger of that – false pride is an emotion that has absolutely no connection with love. At this moment you're the one who matters to him, in spite of everything; you know full well that in a moment, whatever he's thinking or you're thinking, you'll have complete control over him. 'And after all, he does care about me, he brought me some sweets . . . '

All compassion now, Elisa smiled at him, in the darkness barely illuminated by the night-light. Think no more of the snowy road and mysterious fields, or the lights from the neighbouring village and the secrets that might lie there . . .

Let your thoughts slide furtively over those painful images, let them come to a halt at the moment when he held out that little yellow bag. 'He's brought me some caramels . . . ' Give him back that present a hundredfold, offer yourself up to him without restraint. Sliding her hands under the bedclothes Elisa seeks out and caresses that naked body whose every tiny blemish she knows so well.

As they made love she behaved as if there were no weight in her heart, apart from that painful, exhausting happiness that all love brings.

And now? Gilles has turned his back and fallen into a deep sleep. The taste of ashes in her throat, she looks at the eternal blue-green window, at the yellowish glow spread by the night-light. Tomorrow the suffering will go on . . . the searching, the discovering, the hope, the despair, and the ceaseless reminder of the contrast between gestures that are familiar to her and that strange new look in his eyes, shining with a secret light. Gilles no longer loves me; how drab the world.

6

A few days after this Elisa saw Victorine again. It was her day off, Victorine explained, someone was standing in for her at the shop, and that was why she was able to come over and say hello.

Victorine leaned against the kitchen dresser as she spoke. Her face was covered in cheap make-up and she was wearing her fake fox-fur and her big straw hat, the kind that can be worn in winter as well as summer. She seemed to have lost all her freshness, all her beauty.

Elisa observed her sadly. She would have liked to tell Victorine that her false elegance made her painful to behold – but she seemed so proud of her finery! She started to wash the dishes, head bent over her task, listening to her sister chattering away. Then suddenly she interrupted her, saying, 'By the way, I nearly dropped in to see you on Sunday. I was sure that Mother and Father wouldn't have gone out – would you have been at home too?'

'No, I went to see my friend – you know, the one who's just got married – I wasn't back until about eight o'clock.'

'Yes, I know her. Where does she live now?'

'Over there . . . ' Victorine pointed her chin in the direction of the next village. 'You know, further on from the farm, on the new road – they've built a group of little houses there. Do you know where I mean?'

Elisa could see again the fields in the night, and beyond them the mass of lights which all at once loomed big and close in her mind, obliterating everything else. And then she saw herself again at the edge of the estate, on the corner of the new avenue, saw Gilles leaning against the wall, waiting for Victorine to come out of her friend's house.

'Yes, I know,' she said. She awarded herself a point: she'd thought her journey had served no purpose, but those harmless-looking lights separating the whitish fields from the distant darkness had made a definite statement, opening up secrets, illuminating everything . . . It was a long way back to the town from the other end, and the air had been freezing, thick with snow. They must have walked fast, bodies huddled close. Elisa sighed. At least they can't have stopped in such weather . . . that was the only tiny crumb of comfort she could find.

She looks up at Victorine again. The young girl has carried on talking but Elisa doesn't know what else she can possibly have to say.

'Eleven o'clock!' Victorine exclaims. 'I must be off, I've some shopping to do.'

Elisa goes with her to the gate.

'That's good, the snow has completely disappeared,' Victorine says, looking at her narrow little shoes. 'The roads are clear again.'

She is still chatting as she stands in the road. Elisa crosses her arms and leans on the bar of the gate, watching her: in broad daylight her cheeks appear even more made-up than before, and the huge brim of her hat ripples with every movement she makes . . . poor Victorine.

Two workmen come down the road whistling. When they draw level with the women one of them, who has a canvas bag slung over his shoulder, looks at Victorine mockingly. 'Hey, look at her!' he wags, digging his mate in the elbow. 'Who does she think she is – Mistinguett?' They go on their way, still whistling.

Elisa bursts out laughing, her head bent down over her arms. She can't stop. Victorine shrugs her shoulders, haughty, and looks at her sister: 'What a stupid thing to say!' She begins to walk off.

'Take it easy, Victorine,' Elisa says, trying to pacify her. 'See you soon!'

Victorine turns round: 'Bye! I'll see you for lunch on Sunday. Kiss the little ones for me, and say hello to Gilles.'

'I'll do that.' Elisa leans over the gate and starts to laugh again. She goes back into the house, half-sits at the edge of the table, and wipes her eyes with the corner of her apron. Is she ever going to be able to stop laughing? 'Who does she think she is – Mistinguett?' No, she can't stop . . . so she carries on, a little more softly now, with a nervous, heart-rending little laugh.

7

'I'll see you for lunch on Sunday . . . ' When Victorine arrived they got the meal over quickly because they wanted to take the children down to some fairground booths in the village square, before it was time for bed.

At the Flobert shooting range anyone who hit the little ball dancing on the jet of water won a red plastic flower; Gilles won three. They gave the little girls a turn on the merry-go-round, and Victorine threw several rings: she wanted a plaster-of-Paris ornament, but she didn't win anything. Gilles bought two sticks of nougat, one for Elisa, one for Victorine, and a packet of doughnuts for everyone. There was still the photographer's booth to visit. Elisa didn't want to go in but Gilles insisted. Was it that she didn't want to be photographed these days? All right, they'd go for one of those big funny frames – all you had to do was stick your head through the hole: only your head was visible.

Elisa still refused, unable to bear the thought of all three of them in the same picture. She was sad, and the whole square seemed sad to her too – the booths, the lights and all of it. She felt relieved when they decided to go home.

When Gilles spotted a friend he showed him the flowers, saying, 'I won them . . . three at a go.'

Victorine was walking beside him, no longer wearing the hooded tulle cape but a little hat made up of three triangles of black satin with a big pompon on the top: it looked like a curate's cap cocked in her crimped hair. She was walking perched on her high heels, always on the lookout, her narrow, tight coat revealing the alluring shape of her bottom.

She drew Gilles towards her, touching the hand that held the artificial flowers. 'Show me, let's see how they would look!' For a moment she held both hand and flowers against the lapel of her coat.

'They look good there,' he said. 'You can have them if you like.' Victorine tucked the metal stalks of the flowers into the top button-hole.

Elisa was walking a little behind them, belly in front, arms behind, dragging one child by each hand.

For some days now it had been less cold, and the road was full of lights and people enjoying themselves. The fair had only four or five booths but that was enough to give you a festive feeling, to make you want to pick up a bit more than usual at the butcher's or make a return visit to the baker's to buy a fruit tart. People dropped in at cafés, little orchestras played, and there was dancing. They joked as they snatched a doughnut or a long, golden chip from a friend's paper bag. Those who stayed near the booths might have thought that those who moved away were leaving the fête, but the atmosphere stayed with them the whole way back home.

When they got to the gate Gilles said: 'Shall we go on? We could go somewhere for a drink, further up – it's still early.'

Elisa would have preferred to go in – and it was high time the children were in bed – but she agreed immediately.

There was dancing here too. Elisa found a place on the bench at the back between the two children, and Gilles and Victorine sat opposite.

For some time now the beer that was served in bars – more bitter than the kind they had at home – had been making Elisa nauseous. Nothing surprising about that: as long as you know what it is that's making you feel ill there's no point in making a fuss about it, you just drink up.

When Gilles and Victorine got up to dance Elisa didn't miss a single one of their gestures. They moved around her like all the others but as always Gilles stood out as the most handsome man there.

Someone who worked with him at the factory was sitting at the next table. 'Hello there, Elisa!' he said. 'How are you doing?'

'I'm not so bad. What about yourself, what's new?'

'Well, we've made up our minds, we're leaving the

country! Gilles could have come too, it's a shame, a good worker like him . . . '

It was true, Gilles was one of the first workers who had been approached. Elisa thought back to the day when he'd come home with the news. There was a factory doing badly, he'd told her, but it was a very long way away. Elisa didn't know exactly where it was except that it was further than the end of France, beyond the frontier with Italy. Apparently they needed workers there, the best workers they could get, for the ironworks. There was an arrangement between the two factories which meant that under your contract you could go there for several years and then return, with good money in your pocket, and get your job back.

As Gilles explained how it worked, Elisa became more and more enthusiastic. He told how a small estate had been built specially for the workers. They'd live rent-free, and have their own light, pretty little house, with its own garden, and on top of that think of the climate! Sun all the year round, winter as well as summer, wonderful fruit – grapes at one franc a kilo, and flowers galore.

'Might there be mimosas growing out of the ground?' she'd asked. Well maybe . . . why not? The only thing was, the work was hard, and some people said that in such heat . . . but work never killed anyone, even under the sun, Gilles had declared, laughing. He'd put his palms under his armpits and drummed his fingers on his chest. 'What they want is for us workers from the north to go and give them the benefit of our knowledge . . . '

They had gone on talking about it for a long time – what they would find, what he would do – they were exultant. Elisa had put her hands on his shoulders and pulled him into some waltz steps, two or three happy turns round the tiny kitchen, bumping into the furniture. Out of breath but a little calmer now, they'd sat down at either side of the table, not speaking, imagining all sorts of things. Suddenly Gilles had said: 'What about the pigeons? Oh well, I suppose I could bring the oldest one with us, the Red . . . '

'But he doesn't fly any more, he's not worth anything at all!'

'Even so, he's my favourite,' Gilles had said softly, scratching his chin.

The next morning they'd been in a hurry and they hadn't mentioned it again. Once Gilles had left the house Elisa had felt rather strange, as though she were in a weird dream – everything was topsy-turvy. She'd looked at the furniture, the tiles, the garden. The smoke from the high furnaces was swirling up in great yellowish clouds, which slowed down a bit higher up and then dispersed languidly until they were almost invisible, disturbing the air with their greyness and their smells. The trees were not doing well. This summer no leaves had appeared on one of their plum trees: it stretched out its great black poisoned branches at the bottom of the garden. A dull sun gently suffused the greys, yellows and purples of the inhospitable earth. As Elisa looked at her house, her garden, her sun, tears surged up in her, but stopped at her eyelids.

When Gilles came home he said nothing; it was Elisa who asked: 'Did you say anything about going to – what's it called – about going abroad?'

'No,' he said, 'you don't make up your mind just like that – I told them I wanted to think about it. After all . . . ' Gilles passed his hand over his face, ruffled his hair. 'And what about you, have you thought about it?' Suddenly he looked her full in the face, offering up to her his light eyes, filled with a very clear message. She had understood straight away and had thrown herself at him, trembling with happiness.

'Gilles, you don't want to leave either! Then we won't go, will we? We'll stay here!'

They'd walked towards the window and stayed there for a moment, standing, shoulder against shoulder, at the big window wide open to the noxious fumes, each one taking in, with a big circular movement of the eyes, the surroundings that they had so nearly lost.

Yes, it all came back to her. But what good had it all done her? Here she was, sitting in this bar, watching Gilles and Victorine dancing, hearing the boring, mechanical music . . . If they put the proposal to Gilles again, she thought – perhaps they already had – he wouldn't even mention it to her. And yet what would they matter to him now anyway, all the things that had kept him from going abroad before?

Elisa drank her beer in quick little sips so as to finish it more quickly. She responded absent-mindedly to the man who was speaking to her: she was watching the dancers. They came back to the table to rest for a while. Victorine was rather hot; two little damp circles had appeared under her arms, staining the pale blue silk of her dress, and the material was slightly rumpled where Gilles had held her. Her face was pink, her hair dishevelled, and she looked good – she was a pretty girl.

The workmate who was about to leave the country had moved his chair up to the table and they all chatted for a while. When the music started again Gilles was just getting up to dance when one of the young men in the party approached Victorine and said with a funny smile: 'Hey, Victorine, it's my turn this time!' As Victorine stood up Gilles looked annoyed – he moved his chair a bit and sat sideways to get a better view of them. They were moving with a kind of languor: from shoulder to knee their bodies were joined, and when the man spoke to Victorine, his chin brushed her cheek. They were the only people dancing like this – it really wasn't done to behave that way round here.

Elisa spotted it immediately; however, she had stopped watching them and was looking at Gilles instead. He sat there dumbfounded, his eyes heavy with grief, his happiness miserably terminated. Elisa didn't miss a single one of the changing expressions on his face: now his mouth was trembling slightly, now his jaws clenched in nervous irritation. 'He loves her,' she said to herself. 'He really loves her.'

Fearful that annoyance would develop into anger, she tried to talk to him, to distract him, but he barely responded, didn't even turn his head towards her. He was going to lose his temper . . . what could she do? My God, yes, he was going to lose his temper. And lose his temper he did, precisely when she expected him to: she found herself giving a little involuntary start, as when you make an internal gesture without letting it take proper physical shape, at the very moment when Gilles abruptly stood up. When Victorine passed in front of him for the fifth time, he shouted at her in a peevish voice that everyone heard: 'Can't you dance decently?' Before she had time to answer, her partner replied: 'What's going on, are you trying to defend your family's virtue? Give over, Gilles, mind your own business!'

He spoke in a half-vexed, half-joking tone, not knowing how to interpret what Gilles had said. Still holding Victorine in his arms, he prepared to resume their dance. But Gilles dashed forward, shoving Victorine aside and hitting the man in the face: 'I'll shut your mouth for you!'

The man hit him back and straight away someone separated them, as people do, urging them to calm down; but Gilles went on struggling, declaring that it was nothing to do with anyone else, that this was a matter between him and 'that lout'.

Elisa, very pale, had remained seated, one hand on each child as if to prevent them from becoming frightened. She rose, pushing the table back a little to give her room to pass. 'Gilles, I beg you, come and sit down!'

He looked at her with the eyes of a drunken man, as if he were wondering what she was doing there – but this look lasted only a few seconds, and he followed her docilely back to the table. Everyone took up their places again; the owner of the bar came up and gave Gilles a friendly slap on the shoulder. 'You all right now, old chap? What got into you? You don't want to stop young people having a good time, do you? Poor Victorine, I think I well might take a turn with her myself, hey, old chap?'

Gilles wasn't taking in a word of what was being said to him: he seemed to be completely wiped out. His eyes were all wet as he looked at Victorine's hands, now poised on the table.

Elisa thought: 'He's really going out of his head.' What she said was: 'No, I think we ought to go home, that would be best – will you pay for our drinks, Gilles?'

After they had left, Gilles began to remonstrate with Victorine in a plaintive tone. 'No one dances like that . . . no one!'

'What on earth was I doing that was so wrong?'

His voice became more nervous: 'You never try to understand . . . You always have to . . . '

A real lovers' quarrel. Elisa felt out of place.

When they reached the house she pushed open the gate and went down a few steps. Gilles called after her, 'I'll take Victorine home – that's best.' They had already gone. Elisa hadn't expected that: she had thought they'd follow her. She could not speak. Recovering herself, she went back up the steps. The children pulled at her arms, crying: 'Mummy, let's go in!'

'Yes,' she said, 'yes, let's go in.'

She stood there, in front of the half-open gate, with this weight in each of her hands, her mouth taut, her eyes searching the shadows of the road for the couple who were no longer visible. 'A lovers' quarrel . . . everyone knows how that ends.'

The children are asleep, everything is tidy, but Gilles still hasn't come home. Elisa waits for him, sitting in the kitchen, her knees wide apart because the shape of her belly stretches the material of her skirt. Her hands lie helplessly on her large bosom. 'Yes, we've made up our minds, we're going to another country . . . Gilles could have come too . . . ' Now it is too late, now here she is in the kitchen, waiting for Gilles. To be far away, to be here . . .

If only it had been possible to create circumstances different from the present ones, to change their whereabouts in the world, to move from a dark country containing Victorine to a country that was full of sunlight! To have had the opportunity to know other people, other countries, other events, other worlds! To know land that was red and marshy, and golden fields, scrubby or covered in snow; to know gentle green hills, arid, blushing mountains, virgin forests like those in the geography books, and copses where on June Sundays you can pick lily of the valley. Orchards full of apple trees, fields of olives. Tall blond workers, taciturn like Gilles, or small ones, dark and full of verve.

And yet . . . if Victorine was here and now, there were other young girls elsewhere, fair or dark young girls called Berthe, Edmée, Marie. Going from one place to another – is that really the world, or is it rather something very small, invisible, confused, something buried inside of us, something that we always take with us wherever we are, whether we are here, or whether we are there? Whether we are far away or at home?

Perhaps Elisa doesn't think in exactly these terms – and yet that is precisely what she means by her long, deep sighs, her heavy immobility, her dull eyes, fixed on one of the nickel knobs on the stove. Everyone has their own way of thinking.

8

The end of January is mild this year, you might think winter was over already. But February comes to an end with a severe snap of cold – dry cold, no snow, no rain. The earth in the garden is so hard that it echoes beneath Elisa's feet, cracks a little near the sheet of ice that stretches against the wall under the leaking tap. Then it rains, heavily, almost without stopping, for several days on end; and one day, suddenly, the sun begins intermittently to shine, cutting through the rain in great shimmering swathes. It is indeed very strange weather – you never know what will happen next. When the sun spreads gently over the garden, like a fan opening out, sultry flashes of spring rise up from the damp earth. But then clouds start to gather, the shafts of sun close up again and yes, it has turned cold, it's still winter. A quarter of an hour later it's spring again. For Elisa, the signs of love and happiness rising up from the earth bring nothing but sorrow.

There is that long sequence of days when she anxiously awaits Gilles' return, days when she is always on the lookout for whatever affection he still feels for her, however small, days when she discovers that he hasn't been seen at the place where he told her he was going. And there are the nights, indistinguishable from each other, when Gilles is asleep but her suffering keeps her wide awake. She moves her hands towards him, runs them over his skin, leans close to his face very quietly, so as not to wake him: she sniffs out unfamiliar smells on him like a ferreting cat. Then there is the day when, coming down from the bedroom, she catches the reflection below – in the kitchen tiles – of their bodies hurriedly disentangling themselves. And that Sunday when Gilles leaves home early to go to a meeting with his mates from the factory: they are to join up at her parents' house, but when she gets there he's already arrived, and her parents have gone out. Victorine's dress is rumpled and Gilles has that special look on his face that Elisa knows so well. For the first time it affects her with a slight sense of disgust.

There is also the day when he comes home with a little bruise on his lip: her heart will bear the trace of that bruise much longer than his mouth.

Sometimes Elisa wonders whether she shouldn't speak frankly to Gilles or to Victorine, to intervene boldly. But she knows Gilles: he might go away; she feels he's in the grip of something so strong that he would be quite capable of leaving her and going to live with Victorine. Whereas although everything in her life is under threat, hanging by a thread, at least nothing is irrevocably broken: he is living with her, after all, he is sleeping by her side, she kisses him when he comes home, prepares his food, talks to him. As long as he is there, he's still hers. And while the drama remains secret, it's within his power to restore the situation to normal. That is the hope that enables Elisa to survive, to struggle on without weakening; that and her faith in her own love for him, the love that still surges up in her with such force when she hears him walking down the concrete steps . . . .

She is now getting heavier and heavier. When she's been doing housework all day her legs get so swollen that she barely has the strength to walk: these heavy limbs and her exhausted, misshapen body hinder the task that she has set herself. Ashamed of her weakness, Elisa reminds herself that she'll soon be agile, slim, pretty again: her confinement seems to her like a new hope which she waits for patiently, retreating back into herself, a little sleepily, dragging her stiffened body and her stagnant grief.

At last she gives birth. The delivery is long and difficult, but feeling unwell, enduring the pain that separates your legs as if your body were going to tear itself in two, this is nothing to a woman like Elisa: she knows that the suffering will last for only a few hours. This kind of suffering appears, stops, comes to the forefront again, rises up and disappears abruptly, never to reappear. It is somewhat later that the real torture begins, when she is lying in bed, body liberated, face even paler than usual, new baby in her arms.

Every evening Victorine comes in to do the housework and cook Gilles' supper. Elisa hears the two of them down below in the kitchen, hears them talking, moving things around; hears Victorine putting out the plates. But now she hears nothing. Raising her head a little she remains quite still, full of anxiety; her heart is beating so loudly that the repercussion in her forehead blocks the silence. Finally the noises start up again. Elisa lets her head drop; her forehead and her hands are drenched in sweat. She pants a few more times and then calms herself, listening again to the words and footsteps. Later on there is another silence – a long, interminable silence, of which every second marches past in her heart. Will it never end, this silence? Once again her body is soaked, as if she has been seized by a sudden fever. She slips her arm gently from under the baby and with clammy hands clutches nervously at the edge of the blankets. 'Gilles!' she cries out. The cry emerges independently from her anguished heart.

Gilles comes up the stairs. 'What do you want, Elisa?'

'Give me a drop of water . . . I'm so hot.'

She watches him: his face looks quite normal, and he was chewing as he walked into the room. He was eating. They were eating in silence – that was all there was to it.

She drinks a sip of water and stretches full out again in the bed, exhausted. She closes her eyes a little, then opens them again: 'Go and finish your supper then,' she says, in her soft, weakened voice.

In the mornings it's Elisa's mother who does the housework. She comes up to the bedroom several times in the course of the morning, saying, 'Do you need anything, dear?'

'No thank you, Mother.'

Elisa watches her busying herself in the room, putting things to rights, folding sheets, changing the baby's nappy. She says little: there is no point in saying anything, when her delight in having another grandchild, the pleasure she is finding in being of service to her daughter, reveals itself so clearly in her smiling, happy eyes.

Elisa's mother is the only woman in the world in whom she confides, from whom she could seek comfort and succour; and yet again this help is denied her. Just as in the course of that night of revelation she realised that she could seek no help from Gilles, she now realises that no confession can be made to the mother of Victorine.

'We need some more starch for the baby,' her mother says. 'I'll ask Victorine to bring some this evening, and I'll give her some oranges for you.'

'Thank you, Mother, that's very good of you.'

On her daughter's face the old woman can see the broad smile of a contented young mother.

9

In normal circumstances Elisa would have rested for several days, but the very moment she could stand up she felt she didn't want to waste time in bed. That same afternoon she felt a good deal stronger. Gilles was stretched out in the next room, on the children's bed; he was working nights this week. Her mother had left a long time ago, Victorine wasn't to arrive until later, and there was no one to stop her getting up. Today it would be Elisa who would prepare supper for Gilles. She slipped softly out of bed and pulled on some clothes, not putting shoes on for fear that the noise of her footsteps might wake him.

She lifted the baby out of his cradle and placed him on the bed, then took the light wicker basket down to the kitchen and put it on two adjoining chairs before going back up to collect the child. This time, as she placed her foot on the first step of the staircase, she felt slightly weak, no doubt because of the live weight she was now carrying. She walked down slowly, nervously, keeping her other hand on the wall all the way down.

At last, she thought, she could take care of everything herself; she'd had enough of other people looking after her housekeeping arrangements. She pushed a chair against the wall back into its usual place, moved the table slightly so that it was well in the centre of the kitchen, and opened the door through to the next room, contemplating for a moment the polished wood furniture, the feeding-bottles, the orange silk lampshade. This was a room they rarely used, but she looked after it with loving care: every week she polished the furniture, washed the windows, cleaned the floor. It was good to know that there was one room that was always neat, a little more luxurious than the others, so that when a friend turned up unexpectedly one could confidently say, 'Let's go into the front room.' Also, to the right of the window of this room was a door that looked directly over the street, so you could go into it without passing through the kitchen. Today Elisa noticed there was some dust on the furniture: she'd see to that tomorrow.

She closed the door and went to sit for a while next to the cradle. This first effort had rather worn her out – she must take things very easy, sit down for a while between each task. In a few minutes she would feel strong again. She looked at the child. 'My little Gilles, my little Gilles,' Gilles would say as he leaned over the baby, and thinking of that Elisa felt a touch of joy in her heart: he hadn't stopped loving the little girls, and he smiled tenderly at his new child. That was a happy omen, there was still goodness in him, nothing had been lost . . .

'My little Gilles,' she said, too, to the sleeping child, before getting up to prepare the meal.

'What's this, you up already?' Victorine said as she walked in. 'I didn't think you'd be . . . '

'I felt strong enough,' Elisa said. 'You can't stay in bed for ever.'

Victorine was returning the twins – for a few days now they'd been going to infant school.

'Tomorrow,' Elisa said to them, 'you'll leave school at the same time as the others, so you can come home when it's still light. I'm better now, Victorine won't have to put herself out for us any more.'

Victorine asked: 'So I don't have to do anything about supper?'

'No, I've already put the soup on. You know, if you've got anything to do at home, there's no reason why you shouldn't go back there.'

Victorine assured her that she had plenty of time, that she was quite prepared to stay a while. The sewing on the pocket of her dress had come adrift, she might as well mend it if there were a needle and thread handy.

'It'd be better to do it on the machine,' Elisa said. 'Quicker and firmer – I'll do it for you.'

'But you'll tire yourself out . . . '

'Nonsense . . . give it to me.'

Victorine took off her dress, revealing her pale blue

slip, and sketched out a few dance steps. 'Shall we play "Statues"?' she asked the children. She pirouetted two or three times before coming to an abrupt stop and standing stock still in a comic pose for a few seconds.

Elisa saw her sister's naked shoulders, saw her high, round, pink breasts jutting through the broad lacework, saw, under the linen, the outline of her long, slim thighs. She lowered her head and with a bitter surge of emotion moved the material forward under the needle of the machine. Should she speak to her, make her understand that she was in the process of destroying one of the greatest happinesses in the world, tell her that everything might depend upon her behaviour? 'Victorine, you are a woman, as I am a woman, and when confronted by a man's desire you have a choice between all the many different possible courses of action that a woman has . . . '

What would be the point? Victorine would only put on that funny pointed expression of hers and say: 'What do you mean? What have I done wrong?' For Victorine is one of those creatures who have no consciousness of their actions: she parades her irresponsibility throughout her life. One day, simply because Gilles was there, perhaps because it was rather too hot, her flesh desired that man, and she took him. So what? Nothing more in it for Victorine, it stops there. Afterwards it's a question of trying to make sense of things, sense of life, and life doesn't touch Victorine, it will never mark her smile or her eyes, which will stay young, clear, innocent for a long time. Unconscious offenders are the most dangerous of criminals.

Elisa feels strangely ill-equipped to deal with someone like this: how can she get through to her?

It isn't that Victorine lacks intelligence: Elisa remembers that she was always near the top of her class – how else could she measure it? And Victorine has a sense of justice, knows it's wrong that there are poor and there are rich, a sense that Elisa herself doesn't really have: when Gilles tells her about various demands being made by his mates in the union she asks, 'Why are you claiming those things?'

'Because they're fair,' Gilles says.

She throws her head back a little and laughs: 'What do you mean by that word "fair"?'

But as for the case preoccupying her at present, she is well aware that it isn't a question of justice or injustice. She does want to make sense of the fact that Victorine has taken Gilles from her, that she is doing wrong, but the thing that seems to her most monstrous, most inexplicable of all, is that Victorine still manages to preserve her angelic demeanour. There is something missing in Victorine – something oppressed, abused, wounded, even in the heart of evil. It is something that she has possibly managed to overcome, but it exists nonetheless, and it reveals itself deep in her eyes, in every movement she makes. Suddenly Elisa says to herself: 'I believe Victorine has no heart – and that's why it is that life leaves no mark on her . . . '

Perhaps she is right.

It wouldn't be impossible to forgive her for her behaviour, if only there were some sign of wrongdoing on her face at the same time! But no, there she is, svelte, fresh, pure as ever – swaying her pretty, dishonest body around the room, bringing it to a sudden halt in a comic pose, making the children scream with laughter. She is all innocence.

Victorine's dress lies on the sewing-machine table ready to put on but she seems in no hurry; she wants to continue with the game. Elisa picks the dress up and throws it abruptly at her. 'Cover yourself up, for goodness sake!' she says. There is a menacing tone in her voice, for she, Elisa, does have a heart; she knows very well that she is capable of doing wrong and she recognises that surge of hatred which has suddenly stolen up on her, that desire to hit Victorine, to strangle her, to smother her unsupported, artificial life. But she knows how to love as well, and she did love Victorine – suddenly there rises up in her thoughts the image of a clumsy little girl whose attention she's had to divert from the piles of clean washing. She loves her still . . .

She sits a little apart from the others, eyes turned towards the window, where it is just possible to make out the little garden in the darkness. The only feeling left is an overwhelming need to weep.

'Why don't you go off home?' she says. 'There's nothing more you can do to help me, and Mother might need you.'

'I've plenty of time, honestly. Let me wait until Gilles wakes up.'

'Do go, Victorine, Mother was very tired this morning and you can give her a hand . . . I really want you to go.'

Her voice is firm. Slowly Victorine puts on her hat and her coat. She hesitates, a peculiar expression on her face. She hasn't made up her mind to go yet.

'Mother will be worried – I promised her you'd get home early. I'm still quite weak, you know, don't get on my nerves, do please go.'

'All right, all right, if that's what you want . . . ' Shrugging her shoulders, Victorine says goodbye. 'I still don't see what difference it would have made if I'd got home half an hour later . . . '

10

In the week after that, Gilles changed: from being taciturn he became irascible. When he came home, usually late, he scarcely brushed his lips over Elisa's forehead, though she awaited him in the same state of immobility and tenderness as on that very first day. He'd place his blue enamel water-flask on the edge of the window and say: 'At least that's another day over with! I've had such a lousy time.' His brow was creasing and he was losing that fine alertness he used to have, the look of a strong, robust worker. Elisa did her best to be loving and attentive, but she couldn't bring a smile to his drooping mouth, nor inspire an affectionate look in his heavy eyes. His sighs seemed to suggest that he was in a state of nerves rather than in pain, or perhaps his misery had been engulfed by anger.

Elisa had become active in the house once more, working hard and fulfilling his smallest needs even before he revealed them. She managed to look young and happy again. She would try on him either a tenderness that revealed itself openly or a love that was discreet and self-effacing. And she was pretty again now: after the physical lethargy of the last few weeks she'd retained only a slight heaviness of the breasts, swollen with milk, which suited her fine, strong figure. Elisa wanted to feel her big warm body against his breast; longed for an embrace from the arms which now she never felt around her.

There was no class for the children on Thursdays and Elisa made use of that afternoon to do some local shopping. 'Don't touch the little one,' she said to them. 'Let him have a good sleep. I'll be as quick as I can.'

She took her shopping basket and opened the door. Outside she felt that first, gentle warmth that you sometimes get on afternoons in late March. She stopped for a while, looking at the earth. Usually this was when they would have been busy in the garden. Other years at this time, as soon as Gilles got back from work, they'd go into the garden together, and in the growing darkness would point out to each other the buds on the trees, and decide what to sow: a lettuce here, a radish there, and check the state of the little lawn that they kept for the children. 'Better throw a handful of seeds on the children's patch of grass,' Gilles would say. 'It looks worn out.'

This year, even if Gilles did dig, weed and sow as usual, what feeling could Elisa have for the flowering apple tree or the tiny, tender, green shoots which would sprout up from the vegetable mould? She sees herself in previous years, kneeling on the path, her head leaning over the earth.

'What is it growing there, Gilles – carrots or radishes?'

'Guess,' he said. 'If you get it wrong, you better watch out . . .'

She'd get it wrong on purpose, so that Gilles could make fun of her and, still laughing, snatch up the watering-can to shower her with a great spray of cold droplets. She would run away, and he'd catch her, kiss her. 'Gilles!' she'd say. 'Right in the middle of the garden!'

'Why not, you're my wife, aren't you?' And he'd start all over again, even more passionately.

Remembering all that, Elisa shakes her head from left to right and moans: 'Oh my God, oh my God . . .'

The weeks pass and nothing much changes, even though she has pinned so much hope on the birth of the baby. This disappointment rather weakens the courage of the great Elisa: around her, today, everything appears so sad, such a stranger to her grief. If only someone could hear her, could appreciate the weight she feels in her heart; if only someone could advise and comfort her! But who can she talk to? Not to her mother, nor to her sister, nor to her husband. She makes up her mind that during the fortnight before Easter she'll go to church, according to the custom.

She goes back into the house to put on her hat and to warn the children that she'll be away for an hour.

In the square the doors of the church are wide open. Children are filing in; little boys are solemnly uncovering their shaved heads. Others are coming out, scurrying about under the porch around the font, crossing themselves with rapid gestures, clattering down the steps, happy to be in the open air again. Some old women wander in and out, their appearance unchanging.

Elisa hesitates, seized by a strange sense of decency: can she really deposit her secret here, in the very heart of the village? This wound born in the breast of the household and the family, can she disclose it at last, express it for the first time, here between these walls where the children come every Sunday? Can she really free her heart in the very place where she and Gilles were married? No, she prefers to continue along the way. She'll go a little further, to the church in the next parish.

Putting her shopping bag down on the prayer-stool, she knelt down and placed her hands together. There are some women in front of her and she stays in this position while waiting for them to finish. She has never known how to pray: after a very short time she comes back to her own thoughts, absent-mindedly, no longer quite sure where she's got to. Lots of little things come to her mind and interpose themselves between the words of the prayers, putting a stop to their march-past, taking their place before she even realises it. And when she really focuses her attention, makes herself reel off the prayers on her rosary or on her fingers, when she forces herself to leave a clear space in her mind for the words she is saying, she feels that she is abandoning herself to a small, absorbing task which she finds unfulfilling. She is only capable of a single recollection: she thinks either 'God' or 'Jesus' and then, gradually, there unfolds in her mind the image of a great power, confused and shining with light, which for several minutes she loves, without the words and gestures of a prayer.

Today the church is full of sounds and people. A man carries a ladder from the crucifix of the Sacred Heart, covering the images with a purple veil. Someone moves the chairs by her side. Very close to her there rise and fall the whisperings of the faithful and the priest. If she leans forward a little she might hear other people confessing their sins . . .

Elisa unclasps her hands, puts them on the edge of the prayer-stool and raises her head to look around her. There is Saint Geneviève, standing straight on her red velvet plinth with her long flowing hair: you pray to her when you have a sore throat or a nervous breakdown. There is Saint Marguerite, the gentle virgin whose head is weighed down with precious stones: she protects women in labour. Saint Antoine, in a rough, homespun garment with the double oriole of his hair and his golden halo, helps people to find things they have lost. Then there is Saint Roch, eyes lowered towards the dog at his feet. With one hand he lifts a corner of his robe, with the other he indicates, with outstretched finger, the great plaster wound on his knee: he cures people who have been bitten by rabid dogs. Saint Christophe, one foot forward, baton in hand, has a child sitting on his shoulder: you pray to him for a safe journey . . .

And who do you turn to when you are in a state of grief?

At the back of the church Elisa can see a narrow wooden plinth with no flowers and no candles, and on it stands the small, pearly plaster statue of a saint whose name she doesn't know. He has the slim body of an adolescent and he stands in front of a brown tree with no leaves on its three branches. The boy's arms are raised, his wrists joined above his head, his feet barely touching the ground. So insubstantial does his soft, half-naked flesh seem that were it not for the bonds that fasten his wrists and his ankles, you'd think he was rising up from the ground in a gracious pose. With his beautiful, resigned face, his eyes drowning in sadness, this boy must surely be familiar with the whole range of love and of grief. So absorbed is he in his own inner agony that it seems as if he bears the thirteen arrows which pierce him at his shoulders, at his side, at the bend of his arm and at his wrists, almost without pain, rather as if they were mere adornment; they penetrate his body without either tearing his flesh or making it bleed. Instead of wounding him they make him melancholy.

Perhaps because she can identify this boy's unknown, mysterious grief with her own, perhaps because her own flesh is in such a turmoil of love and loss, Elisa is captivated by the little martyr, unknown to her; his young, pink plaster throat seems to her to swell and throb like a wounded pigeon.

Then her turn comes and she goes to sit down behind the green curtain.

She returns to the prayer-stool, picks up the bag she's left on it, and kneels down again. 'For your penitence, you will say a dozen prayers,' the priest said. For your penitence? Oh well, she can think about that afterwards. But already other words are crowding in on the prayers; the priest's phrases echoing in her mind like so many failures. 'In the face of the trials which God sends us, let us beware against any rebellion against him . . . the plans that God has for us . . . Your soul . . . And because you have suffered, later you will . . . '

As if she had ever contemplated rebelling – and what does she care about the safety of her soul and the prospect of life to come! What she needed was help in reconstructing her life on earth, someone to comfort her, to tell her that she had done the right thing up to now and that she should carry on in the same way; she wanted advice on how to bring Gilles back to her so she could finally start to recreate life again.

Elisa sighs deeply, raising her heavy, handsome breasts and looking up again at the adolescent boy covered in arrows, now suffused in tender shadows. There is absolutely no sense of resignation in this sigh which emerges from her passionate flesh, her heart too full of love and of life. With the hope that Gilles will return to her she can still bear his indifference without rebellion. But is she perhaps deluding herself by putting all her faith into this one love? Ought she to be behaving differently in some way? This is what she needed to know, this is what no one has told her. And again she feels alone, at a loss.

Elisa slips her rosary back into her purse with desultory movements and, making her way through the chairs, walks out of the church. How mild the air is outside! The sun has gone down but some gentle sunbeams are still playing around the trees in the main square. Elisa has to go to the greengrocer's, and to the dairy to pay the bill, and she mustn't forget to pick up some sugar, and some soap for the washing – but first of all she goes to sit for a while on the bench beneath the figure of Christ that backs on to the outside wall of the church. She'll only stay for a moment, just to savour the sweetness of this late afternoon, and perhaps to suffer from it a little, for this in-between season fills the air with a curious confusion of memories and fresh delights: as well as promising a new spring, full of life, it resembles the faded springs of the past, forever preserved in the memory of the heart.

She looks round the square at the men, at the women, at the children playing. She watches a tall, fair girl with books under her arm walk past the church then stand stock still on the edge of the pavement, near the iron post which marked the tramway stop, anxiously scanning every vehicle that passed. Three children in funny costumes emerge from one of the roads: the first has a pith helmet on his head, the second is carrying a placard and the third, in a white overall, has a trumpet slung over his shoulder. Is it a live advertising stunt or are they just children playing ludicrous games?

A door opens, a workman comes out and runs across the square. More men, more women, pass to and fro. And in the evening, one couple after another will come and lounge on this bench, at the feet of Christ. Elisa looks at Him, and thinks of how He is watching all the same things that she is; perhaps she might be better understood by this one, who sees life passing by, and who has no doubt seen her too, sitting on the bench, full of love, of pain, of desire, all emotions that are marks of the life He has given her. Now at last she begins to pray:

'Is it true that I have behaved correctly up to now and that I should continue in this manner? And that I should not resign myself, console myself by my suffering? If I continue to love Gilles, if I endure this situation without intervening more forcefully, you must know that it is not through weakness but because I believe it is the only way to keep him for myself, the only way to reconstruct our life. I believe I should continue to uphold and defend my love. But oh my God, if I do this I shall need your support from time to time . . . '

Having said these words, very softly, scarcely moving her lips, Elisa looks up again at the image for a moment. The same dying light steals over her limbs as it does over the wooden polychromatic head and arms of the statue: on the right temple there shine three drops of blood which the carver has made enormous, regular, almost in the shape of a heart.

It is late now, and she still has to drop in on the greengrocer's, the grocer's and the dairy. She gets up and hurries off, so that she will be back home before him.

It was hardly worth the bother, for he was two hours late. He was in a very good mood, for the first time in several days. Elisa worked out that on the other days of the week he had barely seen Victorine, that she had been devoting her time to others, that things hadn't been going well between them; he'd come home early in that irritable mood, face drawn. Today he must have seen Victorine for a while, and no doubt she'd been warm towards him, so that he'd been able to believe she was faithful again. He was happy, he joked, he played with the children – he even talked to her a bit during the course of the evening. So it came about that she, Elisa, was able to take for herself a tiny part of the happiness that Victorine had given him.

11

This good mood lasted barely two days, then Gilles again became nervous, angry, violent even, whenever he was crossed. They were to spend Easter Sunday with Elisa's parents, but when they arrived Victorine had gone out.

'She's gone to enjoy herself with people of her own age,' Elisa's mother explained.

Gilles was at a peak of irritation: he looked at the clock, he watched the comings and goings of passers-by from behind the curtains, he prowled around on the spot like a chained dog. At one point Elisa feared that his unnatural state of distress would arouse the curiosity of the two old people, but they were too preoccupied with the children to notice – besides, she said to herself sadly, how could they possibly guess at the cause? When it was time for them to go, Victorine still wasn't back.

'I ought to go home because of the children,' Elisa said, 'but if you want to stay a little longer . . . '

'No,' Gilles said in a churlish voice. 'I'll come too.'

They walked back through the darkened streets, Elisa carrying the baby, Gilles at her side, the two little girls just in front of them. As they passed the river the twins, just for fun, walked on the very edge of the quay. Gilles pulled them back abruptly, uttering the only sentence he'd spoken in the entire journey: 'Now that really would be the end, if you two fell into the water!'

Elisa called them to her and told them both to hang on to the edge of her coat. They went on their way, Gilles saying nothing, looking straight ahead, Elisa observing his clenched jaw, his hard, embittered face. At that moment she felt real pity for him.

When they got home he sat with one elbow on the table, still saying nothing. Elisa fed the baby, a hand-kerchief stretched over her breast because the little girls were in the room. Then she took the children to bed, continually urging them to behave: 'You must keep quiet, you mustn't make a noise – your daddy is very tired.'

When she came down Gilles hadn't moved, but his arms were crossed on the table, his head leaning on them; he looked like a man who'd fallen asleep on the spot, wiped out by fatigue. Taking advantage, Elisa said: 'Gilles, you've fallen asleep on the table – let's go to bed, my dear, you seemed so tired today.'

She poured out a cup of coffee and put it beside him. 'Come on, have some coffee, it'll do you good.'

He didn't move, didn't reply, but freeing one of his arms, sought out Elisa's hand and squeezed it, in a complete gesture of friendship. Elisa was so moved that she didn't dare speak, for fear of betraying herself; she simply squeezed his hand back. Then she went to sit beside him; at last she could speak. 'Perhaps you've caught a touch of flu – you can't trust the weather at this time of year; it's so easy to catch something.'

He lifted his head; she waited for what was to come.

'I'm not ill,' Gilles said. 'You mustn't worry about me.'

'If you're not ill . . . perhaps you're over-tired?'

Gilles lifted his hand, then let it fall back limply on to the table and continued, under his breath, as if he were speaking to himself: 'I'm done for . . . '

Restraining herself from too loving a gesture, Elisa just placed her hand on his shoulder and said, very simply:

'But what's the matter with you? Tell me . . . '

He looked at her calm, kindly eyes, and was already halfway to surrender. 'I can't tell you . . . but if only you knew!'

She might have said 'I do know' – she might, in revenge, have made him realise with a single blow that she wasn't one of those women who can be deceived, given him a glimpse of the strength of her love and the depth of the suffering she'd been through over the past months. But so generous was Elisa that she wanted to grant him the privilege of confessing.

'Is it an affliction of the heart?' she asked, smiling gently.

She looks at his lost eyes filling up with tears, at the grief which even now can't quite let itself go. Still, she is quite sure it would take very little for him to start confiding in her. And this is a place that she is determined to occupy in his new life, even if it means playing on his weaknesses.

'Cry, it'll do you good.'

Men like Gilles cry in a funny way. He gives out two or three great hiccoughs, almost without tears – enough to make him feel he needs tenderness and consolation; he lets his head fall against Elisa's shoulder. And he talks. Not at all to explain things to her, but to comfort himself; he talks so carelessly, and so naively, that if she hadn't been forewarned she wouldn't have been able to bear the blow. Clearly this suddenly occurs to him because he looks at her and says: 'How can I be saying all this to you?'

Elisa's face is calm, her gentle smile broader, which he takes as continued kindness, encouragement to carry on talking; he doesn't realise that what has transformed her in this way is the joy of victory. She has found the place she was looking for, he has begun to confess, he has spoken her name, revealed the worst. At last, of his own free will, he is going to open up his heart to her.

'Well, these things happen,' she said. 'And if you couldn't speak to me about it, who else could you talk to? You couldn't keep it to yourself, it was like a weight that was making you ill.'

'Yes, it's true – who else could I have spoken to? The truth is that the most important people in my life are her and you . . .'

Elisa accepted the blow without flinching, her smile fading only a little. 'I still count in spite of everything, then, do I? As well as her?'

Gilles responded with an involuntary boorishness, as if that were self-evident: 'You? Well of course you do, you're my wife, aren't you?'

His wife, what did that mean? The woman who keeps house, prepares food, produces children? Elisa wouldn't admit to herself that he was behaving like a pig, and subconsciously put herself on his level, hiding her true feelings out of an innate sense of decency in phrases that seemed to bring the drama back to a perfectly common-place situation. 'Of course – ours is an old story, rather faded now – we live together – we go on making children out of habit – and for the rest I understand that you . . . besides, we can get on well enough like that, don't you see – for us, life can go on just as if there wasn't that, that other thing . . . what worries me is that you seem to be so unhappy – you seem so fretful these days – I had noticed that you were eating your heart out for something . . . never mind, I'm sure that your little, your little . . . affair . . . will be over soon . . . '

Caught in the trap that she had instinctively laid for him, he opened up further, no longer just sticking to facts but revealing his own feelings too:

'Oh but it's not just a little affair, it's . . . '

He wanted to tell her, but it appeared to be too

difficult. For a moment he remained silent, as if he were seeing a series of interior images, then, with a great gesture of the hand which seemed to take in his whole body, he summarised: 'It's like a fire, a great fire . . . '

Still seated, he parted his legs a little, leaned forward, rubbed his knees in small circular movements with the palms of his hands and seemed to be reflecting again: 'Or like a frenzy,' he added in a big, guileless voice.

He went silent again, then said: 'What makes me unhappy is that she's a funny kid, you never know where you are with her.' Having hit upon the root cause of his despair, Gilles expounded upon his sufferings for several minutes, without the need of any help from Elisa.

He told her things she already knew: that Victorine was fickle, that she failed to understand either his pain or his reproaches. Elisa watched him, attentive to every single word as well as to each gesture and facial expression, all of which revealed the depth of his bitterness and showed her yet again the measure of this curious passion that was engulfing him. She suffered silently, like a mother powerless to help, and she kept saying to herself: 'It's like an illness, a terrible illness gnawing away at him . . . '

Suddenly he became very angry, pushing back his chair violently and shouting, 'She's mine, I want her to be mine alone, she belongs to me, for God's sake, she said that herself at the beginning!' Elisa went up to him and pulled his big body against her: 'Calm down, my pet, calm down!' And she pushed back his hair with her hand, touched his brow, as if he were a feverish child.

He let her mother him, they stayed like that. She felt the warmth of his head against her breast.

'You know,' he said, teeth clenched, 'if I caught her with one of those other guys I might kill her . . . '

'What, kill her because she deceives you, remove her from you for ever?' Elisa held him a little more tightly than before. 'You can't truly love her if you say a thing like that.'

Gilles removed himself from her embrace. 'Not love her? That's absurd – not love her? Oh, if only I could explain what I feel for her! And you know, she too . . . Sometimes it's yes, sometimes it's no, but when she says yes, well, really, it's as if she loves me too. Not love her! In that case I wouldn't be feeling what I feel! When she gives herself to me . . . '

Overcome by jealousy, Elisa wanted to cry out 'Where?' but she didn't make that mistake, didn't ask the question that had been torturing her for months.

'When I possess that body,' Gilles went on, 'that body . . . ' Not finding the right words he sketched a human shape in the air in front of him, his hands open wide.

She took his hands and gently lowered them. 'Leave it be, my pet, leave it be, you're hurting yourself.'

But even as she held his hands, clasping them rather nervously against her knees, she could see again the gesture that he'd just made. The hands were there, under hers, pressed right against her knees, but it was as if she had double vision: again she could see them rising up into the air, and the body that they sketched out was very clear, a body made of hot, naked, living flesh, held between Gilles' great, ruddy hands.

She closed her eyes, but that only made her see it even better: her sister's small body, well-endowed but not fat, her high, full breasts and long slim thighs, unadorned by lingerie – 'Shall we play "Statues"?' – the loud, rather shrill but expressionless voice, almost without intonation – 'Do you love me, Gilles?' She could see the body living, moving, swaying between those big brown hands which only a moment before had sketched, in wide, slow, evocative caresses, the curves of an imaginary flesh.

He began to speak again but she was no longer listening. He tried to disengage his hands, which she was still holding in hers. 'Don't hold me so tight . . . Lisa? you're not saying anything. I can't bear any more, give me a cup of coffee, it'll do me good.'

She got up, filled his cup. He saw that her face was pale, her features strained. 'Have some yourself,' he said. 'You look so white – there you go, tormenting yourself on my behalf . . . Still, talking to you about it has probably done me some good. You're the kind of person who understands things – not like her – when you try to make her understand something she looks all surprised and says, "What's got into you?"'

'Yes, I know, but maybe she'll change . . . '

'You think so?'

Elisa shrugged her shoulders and went back to sit next to him, pointing to the cup she had just filled and saying, calmly, as if this evening were like any other: 'Drink up, and then we'll go to bed, it's time you had a rest.'

Sitting there, her arms crossed on her skirt, her bosom dropping a little, her face leaning towards him all beautiful and sad, she had watched him drink. He put the empty cup back down on the table and, seeing that she was observing his movements, said: 'You're a funny woman, Lisa! We come home, I sit down, I see you there, and then, all at once, I don't know how, as if it was something that happened all on its own, I tell you everything. You might have whimpered, made a scene, told me I had to go away, and instead of that you stay there, sitting looking at me, as if you were my mother . . . '

Elisa smiled softly, though her face did not lose its sadness.

'There's another thing,' he went on. 'You mean a lot to me, you know – you, the children, the house and everything. In spite of what's happened I couldn't leave all that, I've already told myself so. It must be the same for you – even after what I've just told you, you'll always be there, just the same.'

'Of course,' she said, 'only . . . '

She meant to say: 'Only you must know that I, I, love you too, for me you are the only person in the world . . . '

But then she thought that if she overwhelmed him with her own love, from now on he would start to regret his confession, so instead she said: 'Only . . . you must always tell me everything, you mustn't hide anything from me – then I shall always be there, I'll wait for you, I'll wait until the thing goes.'

'Yes,' he said. 'Yes, I'll tell you everything, it'll do me good to talk to you about it.'

This frankness started straight away, cruelly, when he added in an enraged, desperate tone: 'But as for waiting until it passes, it could be a long wait . . . I tell you, she's really got me – that's it – I'm done for, like I said.'

That started him off again, and he began to cry almost without tears, with those strange little hiccoughs. He said no more.

Elisa locked the front door, prepared the night-light and turned out the kitchen light. 'Come on, let's go up, after all, you mustn't let yourself go to pieces . . . '

He couldn't sleep – every few seconds she heard him sighing helplessly. She sensed in him the ache of rejected desire, and yet it was not open to her, his wife, to intervene, to slip her whole body between his and the image that haunted him. Lying on the edge of the bed she could only risk lightly touching his face, his shoulders, his chest, in a discreet caress, scarcely disturbing the fabric that deprived her of contact with the body she loved so much. How she wanted to help him!

All at once Elisa felt bold enough, and with a tender, anonymous hand, she gently relieved him of his desire.

12

Gilles had made his confession, and Elisa had assumed her unusual position of confidante. Would it make any difference to her miserable life? Yes – she noticed the change the very next morning. For some time now, breakfast and the preparations for the departure to the factory had taken place in a loaded silence. Today Elisa felt she could look him straight in the eye and say: 'Look, I've put you in a slice of tart as well as your sandwiches.' He thanked her with a smile. A small gain that meant a good deal to Elisa.

And from then on their evenings are different too.

Gilles comes home, puts his enamel water-flask on the edge of the window as usual, hangs his jacket on the coat rack and straight away, by a smile or a frown, gives some sign to Elisa as to whether things have gone well or badly. When the meal is over and the children in bed, he tells her about his day: whether he's seen Victorine, what she said to him, what he can tell from her attitude to him. And Elisa always understands everything, perfectly, even finishing his sentences for him, helping him to express his thoughts. 'She smiled at you sweetly and everything changed . . . as though you could feel confident that she loved you.'

'But no,' she says again, 'You've absolutely no evidence that she deceived you today. Yesterday she didn't turn round again after you parted – you were expecting her to and that's left its mark on you, and during the day when you didn't see her, you imagined all sorts of things just because of this little detail that proves nothing.'

Gilles had never thought of that. Nothing new has happened since yesterday, and his doubts had begun at the very moment he realised she wasn't going to turn round – then they increased, without any cause. He is astonished to discover that Elisa has got it right: she always seems to discern the cause of his low spirits, his sense of unease.

Gilles grieves on account of Victorine, Elisa grieves on account of Gilles, and upon this mutual suffering is their connivance based.

On the days when he has nothing to report, Elisa knows that he will go and sit in a corner of the room, head in hands, and remain like that for hours, without saying a word, with that thwarted look on his face. Then she'll say: 'Come on, let's have a round of cards.'

He jibs at first, then gives in, and they install themselves at the table, opposite each other. It's summer again and the lamp wouldn't be lit yet. The window is open to the dusk and they can hear their neighbours talking and laughing in their gardens. The earth, still heavy from the heat of the day, is beginning to cool down – until suddenly there is silence and it is almost dark; they light the lamp. Elisa gathers the cards together, shuffles them and starts to deal. 'Hearts are trumps – your trick.' She plays with an artificial interest, as you do with a difficult child. She plays until sleep overcomes him.

One night, by pure chance, just masculine habit, Gilles awoke, turned to her and treated her as a woman. Elisa, at the end of her tether, indulged herself, obliterated the reality from her mind, forgot everything that had happened. For just a moment she lived in a world which contained only Gilles and his woman. She paid dearly for this weakness: it was the first time she'd not had the tragedy on her mind and, when reality returned, it wounded her for a second time, as deeply as it had on that very first day.

One Sunday, departing from his usual habit, Gilles didn't announce that Victorine would come to them or that they would go to Elisa's parents, nor did he express a desire to go out on his own. Instead, he said: 'It's so nice, why don't we go and spend the day in the country?'

The preparations were quickly made; they went up into the attic to collect the haversack, made some sandwiches and hard-boiled eggs, and filled Gilles' water-flask with coffee. Elisa moved hastily, rather nervously – she wasn't going to abandon herself yet to the prospect of the pleasure to come; all she felt was a need to hurry, to get as far away from the house as possible before Gilles changed his mind and upset all the plans.

They got off the train about twenty kilometres from the town and walked in the woods, taking turns at carrying the baby. At midday they rested in a clearing, where Elisa breast-fed the baby before unfolding a blanket on the ground and placing him upon it. They unpacked the sandwiches which the little girls ate as they ran around from left to right, coming back every now and again to collect their share. Gilles lay stretched out on the grass, his head on Elisa's knees. After he'd finished eating he stayed in that position, calmly, talking of this and that, without making the slightest allusion to Victorine. Her hand on his shoulder, Elisa looked into his face, scarcely daring to say anything, fearful that one simple word might disrupt this state of calm. Gilles stopped talking.

Elisa remembered one afternoon before their marriage, when they'd come for a walk round here with her family. At a turning in the road Gilles had suddenly pulled her to him and they had rolled about in the bushes, kissing long and passionately. She was wearing a new blouse on which the grass had left green marks, and they'd done their best to clean it before going to sit on a tree trunk, hand in hand, to wait for her parents. 'Do you love me?' 'Madly, madly.' They'd laughed because no one else could have had any idea what they were saying to each other. For the rest of the walk Gilles had to keep his hand on Elisa's shoulder, so that no one could see the marks on her blouse.

Elisa was on the point of asking him whether he remembered, but decided that no, it was better not to say anything. He made a sign to indicate that the sun was bothering him; she raised her hand to protect his face.

Now she is no longer thinking, recalling no more memories. Leaning sideways, her hand raised, her big watchful eyes following the gentle heaving of the man's chest, she stays still, her heart full of fragile tenderness.

Later they continue their walk across the wood, emerging on to a vast plateau which to the right stretches as if to infinity, and on the other side drops steeply down in the direction of the town. Here there are very few trees and the sun is burning hot. Gilles pulls a paper from the haversack and makes a triangular hat out of it, which he puts on Elisa's head: 'See how pretty Mummy looks!'

Laughing, the children demand hats too. 'I'll make some more . . . '

As the road gets narrower they walk in single file; they pick honeysuckle from the bushes and daisies from the path. Now, towards the left, you can see a long way ahead: the chimneys of the tall furnaces and the black cones of the slag-heaps stand out on the horizon. They stop for a moment to look around. Here it seems as though you are on top of the world. Then, one behind the other, with their flowers and their paper hats, they start off again, making their way through the tall, reddish grass.

On the train home, people look at them. Elisa is proud of her beautiful children and of this big, handsome man opposite her. He's gathered the flowers they've collected into a big bouquet which he holds on his knees, a little awkwardly. Elisa will decorate the house with them so that a little of this heavenly day will survive into tomorrow.

If only all days could be like this one, she thinks! So many little happinesses, one after another. Walks in the woods, the warm smell of the heather, Gilles with his head on her knee, Gilles throwing flat stones into a river, on the raised path – 'See how pretty Mummy looks!' Little clumps of grass, green, fair and reddish, stretching out in infinite solitude. Nothing more. Apparently unimportant moments, whose secret Elisa – dumb, silent and abandoned – has instantly grasped, possessing them until they become ineffable.

The train rolls along; the third-class carriage is full, and the bitter smell of sweating bodies mingles with the sweet scent of the honeysuckle. There are women, men, smoking or dozing, children on their mothers' laps; faces that Elisa knows absolutely nothing about. Among these unknown faces is a group: Gilles, his woman, and their three children. Again she is seized by the moment. She wouldn't be able to express it but she surrenders to it with all her senses and all her soul. The wound she carries in her heart, the latent suffering she feels welling up in her, is there to remind her of the fragility of this moment. It must surely be possible for a whole life to be made up of moments of such sweetness, of such significance – but would there be room in the heart for so much happiness?

Elisa is a woman without guile, without pride, without a philosophy; she never asks herself whether there is room in the world for a heart like hers.

From her whole body and soul there is rising up a tragic call towards the ineffable. The group: Gilles, his woman, and the three children . . . Her arms tremble a little around the baby she's holding against her, her face quivers slightly; Elisa is advancing through happiness to annihilation. She has closed her eyes, leaning her head against the side of the compartment. You might have thought her a woman like all the other women there, a little tired by her day out in the country.

The platform was very crowded and Elisa followed behind Gilles, who was holding the little girls by the hand. Then he pushed the children in front of him and, turning towards Elisa, said, 'She'll be really surprised not to have seen me today, it was a good tactic on my part, it might make her jealous. She told me she wouldn't be going out this Sunday; I'd really like to drop in at the house to see if it's true.'

'You're not thinking of going there . . . now?' Elisa said in a wretched, scarcely audible voice.

'Yes, let's go!' And taking the little girls by the hand again Gilles walked quickly on into the crowd.

Elisa followed, her face taut.

When they got to her parents' they found the family sitting outside on chairs, close up against the wall of the house, taking the evening air. Victorine was wearing a pink cotton blouse and a black velvet ribbon in her hair which was tightly waved. Gilles and Elisa walked up to them with their children, their flowers, their been-out-for-a-walk look.

'No, Mother, we won't come in, stay where you are. We only meant to drop by . . . the children are tired.'

'Such a lovely day!' said Victorine. 'If you'd told me you were going to the country, I'd have come with you.'

'Really? You'd have come with us?' Gilles asked, with naive delight. 'If only I'd known!' He fumbled in his bouquet of flowers and pulled out the prettiest stems. 'Here, take these, then it'll be almost as if you had come with us!'

Elisa watched his movements, following with her eyes as the stems passed from one hand to the other.

Flowers of tomorrow, reminder of today – every single little happiness is born and destroyed, one by one.

Back home the children were tired and peevish: they

didn't even stop in the kitchen but went straight up to their bedroom. They left the haversack and their clothes on a chair and put what remained of the flowers in the pitcher on the washbasin.

Once again, inevitably, the moment returns when the others are asleep and Elisa is alone, entirely free with her grief. They have brought back with them from the walk a smell of the earth, of the wood, and of gentle country sweat. Out of this drab, basic mixture of smells rises the clear scent of the honeysuckle they have picked on that vast plateau. The beauty and happiness of the day have been dispelled in a single moment . . . A calm day which would last until nightfall, until the time when, stretched out on the bed by the side of the sleeping man, she could remember the moments without suffering.

'My God, my God, don't abandon me, have pity on me, I was so thirsty for happiness today . . . '

Her head turned towards the far edge of the bed, she weeps little strangled tears, a handkerchief over her mouth so as not to wake Gilles.

13

Time passes quickly when you are unhappy, whatever they say. No reference points mark the progress of time, and no happiness distinguishes one day from another. Only misery; always the same.

'It's autumn already!' says Elisa to herself. She's been living without the love of Gilles for half a year, though it seems like only a day, just one interminable day.

Surprised, she looks at the garden: the earth is looking bare, marked with the first white frosts, and the leaves are dropping from the trees. The morning landscapes are blurred by the fine mists of the north – they drift up from the earth and disappear for a while, then return to diffuse the evening light. No more flowers in the garden, only, climbing up the fence, the fat stalks of some leeks run to seed. She can hardly believe autumn has already arrived – she feels as if she hasn't lived yet.

She moves away from the window and walks on into the kitchen. She looks at the framework of her life: the table and chairs, the staircase leading up to the bedrooms, the stove and the sideboard. Who cares if the seasons come and go? There is only this misery that seems to have no end. For months now Elisa has been awaiting the dawn of a new day.

Returning to the thread of her thoughts, she finishes by saying to herself, 'Autumn already! How slowly the hours pass!' The only time that counts is the time of the heart.

Although Elisa had been up for some time, Gilles hadn't yet returned from the factory. She no longer stayed in bed until he came back when he was working nights. She crossed the small room with its waxed furniture and opened the front door. The mist was still too dense, she wouldn't see him coming along the road. She went in, came back with a broom, and began to sweep the little stone pavement. Suddenly Gilles loomed out of the fog, right next to her. 'Lisa!' Without any further sign of greeting, he went into the house. She followed him.

'Do you want to eat straight away?'

'Yes, I'll wash later.'

She served him a cup of hot coffee, then sat down at the table opposite him, and had something to eat herself. He didn't say a word. Because of the cold air outside, the window was closed, and a smell of fried bacon filled the room. Everything seemed empty, piteous, in the early-morning light. Elisa felt stifled. To break the silence, she said: 'We ought to pull up the leeks that are still worth eating, otherwise they'll run to seed like the rest.'

'If they run to seed, they run to seed.'

Better not to insist. The day was not starting well. Yesterday evening Gilles had been quite calm – but no doubt during his night shift he had given birth to all sorts of suspicious thoughts; she just had to suffer the consequences and hope that they went away of their own accord or that Victorine gave him a hopeful word or gesture. Elisa had even come to the point where she hoped that this word or gesture would come as soon as possible – but the thought lasted only a second, and immediately she blushed for having had it. It was difficult: always this bad temper, these sudden flare-ups, these heavy, stifling silences that she could not break with impunity.

These days, confiding in Elisa no longer provided Gilles with the comfort it once had. Victorine had wasted no time in removing this small solace from him: in just the same way as she had once taken pleasure in arousing his desire, she'd now taken it into her head to make love to another man. Lucien Maréchal had a tobacco and cigar business in town, and she was going to marry him. Displaying her manicured hands, her gold band, her fine pearl-and-silver ring, Victorine would hold out little cedar cigar boxes to the customers: 'What would you like, sir – Claro, Cogetama, or Voltigeur?' One idea just like another. And so easy to put into practice: if you're sexy, why not make as much use of it as you can?

Why not indeed? Just carry on, you dirty little bitch. There's no danger in your life, nothing to lose, nothing to gain. Nothing could either raise you up or bring you down; you're a woman who holds on to neither heaven nor hell, a woman with no soul, no heart, no spirit – no flesh even, for you take neither suffering nor happiness from this overpowering sexuality that eats you up. And it's a part of this tragic innocence that makes you go on seeing Gilles, in spite of everything. 'After all, he's a good-looking fellow, that husband of Elisa's!' You walk along the streets of the town, making the most of being seen hanging on to the arm of this handsome blond worker. The tormented, unsuspecting man asks: 'Do you love me, Victorine?' And you, with that special movement of the eyebrows, say: 'Of course I love you! Why shouldn't I love you?'

Your body is adorable, your legs long and white, your skin softer than that of most workers' wives. No great worry, no overwhelming happiness has ever marked your face; your belly shows no stretch-marks. This naked body that Gilles feels against his own seems beyond his wildest hopes, like a creature from another planet. And you, Victorine, you know just how to fake being in love. Your eyelids never close, they blink no faster – and your empty eyes, without knowing why, drive the man to exasperation, haunt him long after he has left you. Lacking real evidence – which he wouldn't have acknowledged anyway – he no longer possesses the confidence of a man who is master of his prey.

In the clean, sad kitchen, life beats almost imperceptibly. Gilles has finished eating his bacon and eggs but stays at the table, eyes full of misery. Your sister Elisa is standing near the window, her gaze lost in the northern mist which, little by little, unveils the black horizon. She can do nothing for you – or against you. No one can do anything, either for you or against you. Rather inhibited by this overwhelming love of hers, Elisa waits. She waits for Gilles to be cured. She knows that one is not cured of Victorine by force, only by disgust.

Elisa went upstairs to get the little girls. She'd wash and dress them in the kitchen, so that if Gilles decided to go to bed there'd be no noise in the bedroom – the baby wasn't due to wake for another hour. When she came down again he had left the table. Slowly he took off his shoes and threw them over to the stove. Then he said: 'I'm going up to try and get some sleep. See you later.'

As soon as he'd left the room one of the twins nudged the other and said, 'He's in a bad temper today!'

Suddenly Elisa's hand struck the child's cheek.

The little girl didn't cry straight away. For a moment all three looked at each other in silence. Astonished by what she had done, Elisa didn't move. Then she took the child in her arms and comforted her. 'Don't cry, darling . . . did I hurt you? But you know, you really shouldn't talk about your father like that.'

Time to leave for school. The fog had completely cleared and a white October sun lit the road. The little girls walked without saying anything, one hand in Elisa's, the other holding their brown cloth satchels. Something funny was going on: they didn't know what it was, but it was something in which they felt they played only the very tiniest part.

On her way back, Elisa stopped at the grocer's. She was in a hurry, so she was served first; it seemed to her that people were looking at her strangely. As she went out with her shopping one of the women inside spoke too soon: Elisa heard her say, 'What a carry-on! And she must know about it, don't you think – you can see it in her face.'

So, people knew. That was inevitable: it was enough for them to be seen leaving each other on the road, taking too long over their goodbyes, for people to start taking notice. Perhaps they'd been seen in the woods, or behind narrow hedges. Hidden by the shelves which decorated the shop window, Elisa waited a moment, then heard the other woman reply: 'As I see it, if she puts up with it she's not much better herself.'

Elisa set off again, her big black scarf crossed over her chest, her arms full of shopping. Her heart was beating fast, but she dawdled along past the hedges, the low garden fences, the narrow brick houses. Her body was bowed and her face looked as if something had suddenly just died in her. She pushed open the door of the kitchen and sat down on the nearest chair, opening her arms,

:tting the shopping fall on to her knees. She fixed her eyes upon an empty corner of the room. Then, one by one, she picked up the shopping bags and put them on the table. She took off her scarf, shrugged her shoulders: after all, it was only a very small thing by comparison with all the other blows.

Gilles came down at about eleven. As he wasn't wearing shoes she didn't hear him coming. Taken by surprise, she stayed like that, looking at him, a tea-towel in her hand. He bent his knees so as to be level with the narrow mirror hung on the wall and tidied his hair with his hands. Then he sat down, put his shoes on and finally said: 'No chance of sleep, so I'm going into town – I know she sometimes gets it into her head to drop in at Maréchal's in her lunch-hour.'

Elisa searched wildly for some reason to stop him going. Standing in the doorway, she instinctively placed her hands on the door-frame, barring his passage with her outstretched arms.

'But Gilles, you must rest! What kind of a state will you be in for work tonight?'

'I'm not going to be able to sleep! It just came to me that she might be going to see him in her lunch-hour today. If I don't check I'll go out of my mind.'

Elisa's arms dropped to her side and she felt his big body brush against hers as he passed without stopping.

*

Two hours later he was back.

'I stopped by Maréchal's shop,' he said, 'and left when I was sure that she wouldn't be coming. I could have gone to look for her where she works – then I would have been sure of seeing her, but I wouldn't have known what she was planning to do, would I? This way, if she tells me tomorrow that she didn't go to Maréchal's at lunchtime, at least I'll know she's not lying to me for once . . .'

Elisa went pale. If only, she thought, if only he'd seen Victorine going into the shop, he might have returned more tormented than ever, angry but at last ready for disgust . . . But here he was, triumphant, mollified, tender almost.

'What about those leeks of yours, Elisa? Would you like me to go and dig them up before going back upstairs?'

And on the next day, or the days that followed, Victorine, whatever else she did, would still find words and gestures to hold him spellbound, to keep him within reach, to slake her thirst.

'Don't bother,' Elisa replied after a moment. 'You need to rest, you've got to work tonight.'

'You're right,' he said. 'Perhaps I'll be able to sleep now.'

He went up and she went back to her tasks.

She stood in front of the window to get her breath

back. Lost in thought she let her gaze wander beyond the garden fence over to the little meadow beyond, where her eyes followed the moving shapes without seeing them. Some soldiers on manoeuvre were crawling about in the grass. One of them, crouching very close to the garden, turned towards her and smiled. Their eyes met and he blew her a kiss, just a bit of fun. When she made no movement in response and her face stayed impassive, he pouted at her reproachfully. From a distance it was hard to make out his body, enveloped in a material that merged with the ground and the reddish grass; she could only see his young face, under the helmet pushed back on his head. She smiled back at him. He sat up, detaching himself from the earth. His body was still like a boy's, as youthful as his face; he was too heavily encumbered by material and leather. He gestured to her that he would like her to come and lie beside him in the meadow. He stretched out his hand, indicated the patch of grass next to him, laughed, and brought his arms back towards him, in a movement that suggested an embrace.

Elisa moved away from the window. She could feel her breasts swelling beneath her dress; she covered her face in her hands. Deep inside her she saw only the image of the man sleeping in the bedroom above her.

Climbing the steps gently, she stood and looked down at him. He hadn't taken his clothes off; his big, strong body was spread out all over the blankets. The blue twill of his trousers fitted tightly against his left leg, folded beneath him; she could see its outline right up to the groin. Beneath his shoulders his big hands clung to the collar of his shirt as though he'd fallen asleep in midmovement, revealing the tuft of unruly hair at the centre of the two brown, nearly black, haloes. She watched his powerful jaw, shadowed by yesterday's beard, slacken a little and then contract again. His thick, fair locks were thrown back, exposing his forehead, too pale and speckled with red.

Elisa had never looked at him so closely, had never loved him so much, had never desired him so intensely, with such a tragic passion, with such deep distress in every inch of her body. She stood there, her back to the wall, tense, her skin a little moist, her nipples hard.

Then, at last, she walked away, noiselessly, on tiptoe.

From the kitchen window she watched the outline of the men running away, bent over, guns in hand, down the slope of the meadow. The grass by the garden fence was empty and rumpled: the young man had left to join his comrades. Summoned by them, indistinguishable from them, the man-child had gone back to join in the game of war.

The surrounding area regained its tranquillity; from time to time you could still hear a harsh voice issuing orders, breaking the afternoon silence. She closed the window, rolled up the wax tablecloth on the kitchen table and began to peel the vegetables for the evening soup.

It had been dark for some time, and the children were in bed. The meal was over and Gilles was reading the evening paper. Elisa made his sandwiches, three with scrambled eggs and three with ham, packed them up, gave them to him. He left, and everything died around her.

She stayed idle for some moments, enduring her solitude. From time to time she heard the noise of workers making their way to the factory, coming closer and then fading away. Sometimes they walked in twos or threes and the indistinct sound of words would reach her. Other women would be without their man tonight – but they'd be able to keep the taste of a full goodbye kiss on their lips for a long time, and in their breasts the memory of a big open caress – a faithful, warm, friendly hand brushing against their blouse at the moment of parting. In the middle of the night, feeling the empty place at their side, they might wake, but would know that in the morning, at dawn, their arms would embrace their returning man, as she had once embraced Gilles. Bodies that were hungry but without anxiety, that would be happy and fulfilled in the first sun of the day.

Elisa clasped her arms around her and leaned her head on her chest. A solitary night, a tomorrow without hope.

A unique day, with no other day in sight. 'It just occurred to me that she might be going to Maréchal's in her lunch-hour today' . . . 'I could have gone to look for her where she works, then I would have been sure of seeing her' . . . 'As I see it, if she puts up with it she's not much better herself' . . . 'If I don't check I'll go out of my mind.'

She lifted her head and sighed, tidied up the kitchen, put out the lamp, climbed the stairs.

For a long time she stood at the bedroom window. In the darkness she could just make out the undulating shape of the meadows, then further on the great square of empty night. Further still shone the foggy lights of the factory, the furnaces lighting up the sky with red. The siren blasted out the hour, marking the change of shifts: he was about to start work.

14

At seven o'clock the next morning Gilles had still not returned. Elisa had been worried for some time. She began to dress the children, keeping an eye on the window for the slightest sound from outside. At this hour in the morning it seemed very unlikely that Gilles was with Victorine. She feared an accident. Panic-stricken, she had visions of Gilles crushed beneath a steel bar or trapped in the steering mechanism of a monstrous machine. There is no recourse against that kind of misfortune. And as she busied herself with her housework she was quickly praying that the delay was caused only by Victorine.

It was past the time when the children ought to depart for school but she couldn't bring herself to leave the house. Finally she made up her mind to go. Reassuring herself that the baby was sleeping peacefully she went with the girls some of the way, then left them, telling them to walk sensibly on the pavement. Her hand on her forehead, she watched them for a moment, waiting until they'd crossed the square. If Gilles hadn't come home when she got back, she'd run as far as the factory. As she turned her gaze away from the girls, she saw him suddenly. He'd just got off the tram and was coming towards her.

'What's going on, Gilles? You had me really scared.'

He looked tired; although it wasn't hot, sweat was pouring down his face, mingling with the night dust.

'I had to see her, so I followed the road she takes to get to the shop. She was wearing a necklace I didn't recognise; she looked weird to me.'

Elisa didn't answer. He was back at last, he was walking beside her. For a moment she gave herself up to the heavy feeling of happiness that follows on from anxiety.

She raised her head towards him, touched his arm. 'You went into town like that, all dirty?'

She looked back at the road again and went on, in a lower voice: 'Gilles, you're being clumsy. You're going to end up by getting on her nerves if you keep on following her like this – it'll look as if you're running after her. What will she take you for?'

'It's only natural,' he said animatedly. 'Whatever she's done, she must know very well that she belongs to me, after everything that's happened between us!'

'Don't see her for a bit, keep your distance,' Elisa said softly. 'If you pretend to be indifferent, if it looks as if you've left her, she'll realise she's behaved badly, and she'll come back to you of her own free will.'

Elisa knew she was playing a dangerous game but it seemed to her that the time had come to try it. Staying away from Victorine for several days might make his need for her grow even stronger, but it was equally possible that Victorine might not realise that his indifference was fake. If Victorine thought the game was lost, she might stop throwing herself at him, might even turn away completely. Then perhaps Gilles would finally realise what the young girl's feelings about him were.

Gilles hadn't said anything, but Elisa's words were circulating gently around his head. He needed time to get used to a new idea.

They'd been home for a long time before he said, without preamble: 'You might be right, you know.'

He said no more, but went on eating with stiff movements, his arms apart, his body too far from the table, holding his bread in his fist. Finally he completed his thought: 'Yes, that's the thing to do, it'd be best if I make no move for a few days, then we'll be able to get a good idea of what she will do. The only thing is, I don't know if I'm going to be able to stick it, getting no news of her at all . . . '

Afraid that in the end he might not follow her advice, Elisa replied, in a slightly oppressed voice, fixing him with a look that she hoped was full of confidence: 'Give it a try. And if you really can't bear being away from her we'll go to my parents' house on Sunday – that way you'll be able to see her, but you won't be alone together. Try to be patient, make an effort!' She added, as simply as she could, 'I'll help you to wait.'

He nods agreement – he accepts her advice! She looks

at him; he hasn't the strength to say a word, he's really exhausted. That walk across town, straight after his work, instead of coming home to rest . . . Gilles works too hard; he ought to have a more ordered life. When a man's life is out to work, return home, eat, sleep, out to work again, he needs to keep it in order or his body loses all resistance. These days, it's as if he's continuing to work whilst suffering from a grave illness. But I will cure him, I will cure him, Elisa thinks to herself, while out loud she says, in a voice full of anxiety: 'You ought to have been in bed ages ago, Gilles. Go upstairs, now, go and sleep.'

Several days passed, without incident.

On Sunday afternoon Gilles shaved and dressed with more than usual care. He had his jacket and his cap on before Elisa was ready herself. 'Come on, let's be off!'

It wasn't possible to walk fast with the children. 'It'll take us too long to go on foot,' he said. 'Let's take the tram, I won't smoke for a while to make up the cost.'

Victorine came in late but Gilles didn't ask her where she'd been; he hardly spoke to her or looked at her. He seemed pleased with himself, and gave Elisa conspiratorial looks.

As they were leaving, Elisa's mother, wanting to help her with her housework, reminded her to bring over the washing. Victorine interrupted: 'I'll come and pick it up from you, Wednesday or Thursday.'

'Don't bother,' Elisa said, seeing that Gilles was not listening. 'I'll bring it myself.'

'No, I'll come and get it.'

As Gilles was coming up to them Elisa didn't respond to Victorine's last sentence.

On Tuesday she began to dread Victorine's visit, and in the afternoon decided to go over herself, so that the young girl would have no excuse whatsoever for turning up. In some haste she packed up the washing in a sheet, tying it up in knots, took the children to her neighbour and left home before Gilles returned.

'You shouldn't have put yourself out, dear! Victorine said she'd drop in at your house today while she was out doing an errand for the shop – in fact she must be there at this very moment.'

Sometimes bad luck is so disturbing that it is hard to take in at first. But Elisa quickly pulled herself together. 'Got to rush, Mother, must get back to the children, can't stay.' She ran all the way to the tram stop.

15

'Tart! Whore! Filthy fucking tart!' . . . I'll hold your face in both my hands and crack your head against the tiles . . . then I'll wait a little . . . to see what that does to the expression on your face . . . Oh, you were so pleased with yourself a little while ago! . . . Why shouldn't you marry him! I'll tell you why you . . . 'Oh my God, oh my God . . . ' and now I'm starting to thump you again . . . with clenched fists, on your forehead, on your eyes, on your mouth . . . You're bleeding . . . it's like a red flower blossoming out of your lip and flowing gently along your teeth . . . Those pretty teeth of yours that want to bite my clenched fist . . . but making no more of a mark than the mouth of a little cat . . . No point in crying out, there are gardens between us and the neighbours . . . 'Shut your mouth! The doors are locked!' My knees are pressing on your thighs, my elbows are on your arms . . . and my hands are around your neck . . . Your whole body is flat on the floor . . . I could have you in any way I wanted you without your being able to make the slightest movement . . . 'You want me to make love to you? I'd much prefer that . . . ' I spit on your face . . . my hot spittle all filled with my anger . . . Don't bother to try and clean yourself up . . . it's not worth it, I'll only start all over again . . . Look at you, you're all spangly, you adorable dirty little creature . . . 'You're only a filthy bitch, you hear me, a filthy bitch!' My teeth are bared, I am in torment, I am panting, I am terrifying you . . . 'But you're not going to marry him, I'll kill you first!' You follow my eyes as they rest for a moment on the poker hanging upon the bar of the stove . . . There's no point in clutching my clothes like that, I can get there . . . I'll drag myself along, pulling you with me . . . but it'll take some time, because I don't want you to get free . . . to escape . . . And I want to hit you again . . . This time I hit you really hard . . . my thumb-nail has slipped on your forehead peeling off a little trail of skin . . . Go on, struggle, weep, cry out, bleed . . . If only you knew how much pleasure it gives me to hit you while you are squirming under me like that . . . I beat you, smash you, hit you, claw at you, smother you, mangle you to pieces . . .

'Bitch! Filthy whore!' These were the words Elisa heard as she passed under the kitchen window. In just three bounds she was at the top of the brick steps.

She pushed open the door and saw the monstrous shape of Gilles, splayed out in a semi-circle over Victorine's small body. Grabbing him by the shoulders, she pushed him back and helped her up. 'Where does it hurt? Is there any serious damage?' She ran her fingers over Victorine's poor, dishevelled body, astonished at its sudden liberation.

Gilles stood there, not making another movement, still furiously, mechanically, mumbling insults. Elisa had gone pale – a paleness which, under her brown skin, made her look livid. Pushing Gilles into a chair she said, 'Sit there, don't move.'

She double-locked the door and put the key into her coat pocket before going back to Victorine. 'Can you walk? Come on then, let's go upstairs.'

She stretched her out on the bed and took off her dress. There were bruises all over the place, her upper lip was swollen, and she had quite a deep scratch on her forehead, but nothing really serious.

Elisa washed the bruised areas in cold water and got a phial of iodine tincture out of the cabinet above the washbasin to treat the wound on her forehead. Victorine screamed unreasonably. 'Try and rest now,' Elisa said. 'There's nothing to worry about, I promise. Stay there and try to calm yourself. I'll come up again soon.'

She waited with her a little while longer, leaning against the end of the bed, while Victorine groaned and cried loudly, blowing out her lips like a child.

Back in the kitchen, Gilles was just as she had left him. She got out a glass and a bottle with a drop of gin in the bottom: 'Get that down you.'

She said nothing more. She came and went in the

room, pretending to be doing the housework. Once she turned her head away; her eyes had filled with tears – she had a physical need to weep. Panting a little, she managed to control herself.

She returned to Victorine, who said that she was feeling better; she could get up now, go back home.

Sitting on the edge of the bed, Victorine put her stockings on, stretching the silk carefully over her pretty legs. 'What a brute!' she said. 'All that fuss just because I told him that I was going to marry Maréchal! I really don't know what got into him!'

'I do,' said Elisa softly.

Victorine raised her head and looked at her in astonishment, then pretended she didn't know what her sister was talking about. She went over to the mirror to do her hair and when she saw her lip and forehead, said again, 'What a brute!'

While Victorine finished dressing, Elisa went back downstairs. She handed Gilles the front-door key and asked him to go and fetch the children: 'They're with Marthe. Why don't you stay there for a few minutes?'

'All right,' he said tamely.

She went back up to collect Victorine and let her out by the door which opened on to the road. 'I'm worried you won't have enough strength,' she said. 'I'm going to come with you some of the way. When you get home, tell Mother that you fell down the stairs.'

The young girl didn't reply. Elisa went with her as far as the tram stop.

Back home she found Gilles, the twins and Marthe, with the baby in her arms, in the kitchen. 'I wanted to bring the little one myself because Gilles was shaking so much . . . I'd say he's had a drink or two!' Marthe said, laughing.

As no one said anything, she went away.

The little girls sat down to their meal; every noisy move they made, every word they uttered, seemed strange.

Now Elisa and Gilles are alone. 'Aren't you eating anything, Gilles?'

So – does life go on? He spreads both hands wide on the table and weeps for what he has just lost, his face open, making the ugly grimace that men have to make to let tears flow.

Sitting opposite him, Elisa slips her hand along the table until it meets his and, giving up at last, mingles her own tears with those of the poor wretch.

16

The next morning Elisa went to her mother's house. Victorine was finishing her lunch. She still wasn't feeling very well and hadn't been to work. Her mother was standing up, next to her. As Elisa came in the old woman turned towards her and said: 'Aha! So here you are!'

Elisa was surprised by the tone of her voice and said, hesitantly, 'Is Victorine better? I was so sorry that . . . '

Their mother interrupted in a cross voice: 'He made a fine mess of her, that husband of yours!'

Distraught, Elisa looks at Victorine. What has she said? Has she told the whole truth? The young girl goes on slowly buttering her bread, without raising her head.

Her mother might know what had happened the previous night but she doesn't know the real cause of the scene because she goes on, in the same tone: 'Can you imagine such brutality! What does he have against this Maréchal? Nothing at all! Just poking his nose into our family business! It's up to your father and me to decide whether this marriage is suitable or not! He's really crazy, your Gilles . . . a crazy man on the loose! I'm sorry for the children having such a father. And if you put up with it, that's your choice – just make sure he never sets foot here again! And what were you doing yesterday evening, why didn't you bring her all the way home? You're a bit much, you and your brute of a husband . . . I would have thought you had more heart than that. Really, it's all quite beyond me.'

Pale as death, her body shaking, Elisa listens to the torrent of her mother's anger. Head bowed, eyes distracted, powerless, she endures the part that she is destined to play.

Beside herself with fury, the old woman marches out of the room. In the strange silence that follows Elisa finally speaks, in a sad, smothered voice. Victorine has said Gilles had beaten her up – does she feel no shame?

'Oh, I know you wanted me to let him off the hook,' Victorine says, sniggering. 'You wanted me to tell some story about falling down the stairs . . . honestly!'

'Mother wouldn't be in this state now if you'd only . . . How can she possibly understand what happened? And what's more,' Elisa adds dully, 'for those who know the truth, it would have seemed more straightforward on your part if you had . . . '

'The truth?' Victorine asks. 'What truth?'

Breathing faster, as if she were taking Victorine's shame upon herself, Elisa murmurs desperately: 'I know what's been going on between you. I've known everything for months and months.'

Victorine looks at her in amazement. For a long

moment both women are silent. Elisa waits for a word of remorse, a sign of affection. But Victorine has waited this long only to say, 'Oh well, my dear, if you knew what was going on, you should have kept your husband at home!'

Elisa stifles a cry. She wants to speak, to scream out her hate and her scorn; she utters not a word. Shoulders sagging, face dead, she turns towards the door. Their mother comes back in, and without looking at Elisa, sits down by Victorine.

Elisa looks at both of them, sitting next to each other. Victorine lifts her hair with her hands to show the bruise on her damaged forehead.

'Eat up, my child, you need to after all you've been through!' Concerned, the mother passes the bread and butter across to the young girl. This is all right; Elisa understands. Everything is logical, normal, painful and unchangeable. She has nothing to say, nothing to explain.

Should she expose Victorine? Could she reveal her empty heart to this mother of hers; defend herself, explain herself? Should she tell her about the love she felt for Gilles? But what words could she use? Anyone looking into those tender eyes who really wanted to understand would have had to scrutinise her swollen heart, to search deep into her loving flesh, in order to discover even a morsel of the admirable secret that permeates every fibre of her being.

But she is there, at the other side of the table, still watching the two women sitting side by side.

She has nothing more to say . . . nothing more to do here. Her place is elsewhere, with Gilles. How she is going to have to help him, to support him!

She gets up and looks at her mother, sitting there quite still. For a moment she closes her eyes and feels within her the memory of a cool hand touching her forehead during childhood fevers.

Out in the road she walks on, with a look that is fixed and wild, her big black scarf floating on her shoulders.

17

That evening Elisa told Gilles what had happened in the morning. He let her speak without interrupting, his face marked by unchanging desperation, as if he wasn't listening to what she was saying. At last he spoke.

'Ever since yesterday all I know is she doesn't love me. Apart from that I don't know what's going to happen.'

Elisa felt afraid, and said abruptly: 'You mustn't go back to her! Don't take her back, don't punish her! Do you hear me, Gilles?' She shook him, trying to reach his bewildered brain. 'You're lost, you must wait until your grief eases, you mustn't do anything else at the moment!'

She added more quietly: 'You're very unhappy, but you're not abandoned. You must know . . . '

She seemed to collect herself and went on, modestly, as if offering him meagre consolation, 'I love you, you know, Gilles. I love you passionately, as I've always loved you, as if I'd been born for that alone . . . '

He looked at her vaguely, as despondent as ever. Then slowly, from the very bottom of his memory, a recollection began to emerge from long ago – why this one and not another? he wondered. One Saturday evening, after work, he was sitting outside a café with three of his mates. The young workers winked and nudged each other and said, 'Look, here comes lovely Lisa!' She is walking along the crowded street and her tall, graceful body passes so close to them. Her eyes look directly into his, into his alone. For days on end, the flame of that look stays bright in his heart.

And as if, for the first time in months, he were regaining awareness of the woman who lives with him, he says: 'Yes, Elisa, I know you love me, I do know. And I've behaved like a complete swine towards you.'

'If you say that yourself, it means there must be more to you than that,' she replied with a forced smile.

She thought that something tender was about to cross his face but he was already opening his arms in a gesture that said, 'None of it makes any difference.'

He didn't say another word that evening.

The days that followed brought a cold, heavy rain. Narrow gulleys soaked the sloping garden paths, and the last autumn flowers, drenched in water, rotted without fading. In front of the kitchen, on the brick steps, the concave part never had time to dry out and was constantly filled with rain, splattering the low doorstep, seeping in under the door. Elisa stuffed the gap with an old, folded-up bag. 'This is rain made to last,' she said to herself, frustrated because the children had to stay shut up in the kitchen, getting on Gilles' nerves with their games and their talk. In the evening, gusts of rainy wind blew violently down the chimney, beating back the fumes which swirled up around the lid of the stove. As soon as they opened the window, the room was filled with a glacial humidity. Gilles and Elisa would sit next to one another in this trapped air. Elisa would place her hands on his, and he would tell her about his sad thoughts.

She no longer said anything about herself, about her own love: she would listen to the long complaints, interrupting only with a comforting word, a reassuring gesture. Her whole being radiated tenderness. Her watchful eyes were a living support to him, her tender, throbbing flesh an offer of consolation. Elisa concerned herself only with Gilles and Gilles only with himself. She told herself that he would be helped by this constant, imperceptible care with which she'd subtly managed to enfold him.

And in fact she did help him.

Gilles got better.

The rain had stopped and the warm weather was back. There were still some storms, strong, heavy rumblings of thunder. In the evenings a red sun lit up a congested sky – the last sign of an autumn dying in its own beauty.

The geraniums came back into bloom; a single late rose flowered, and Elisa picked it. The vases were all too big for this one bloom so she put it in a glass, on the table, ready for Gilles' return.

When he came back he'd sit on one of the concrete steps. Elisa would join him, and they'd stay for a long moment side by side in the vanishing light. Sometimes Gilles would say, pointing at one of the faded borders, 'Next spring we'll sow some mignonettes.'

'Yes, they don't have much colour, but the smell is so lovely!' Elisa would reply, her voice heavy with restrained happiness.

Then, suddenly, Gilles was overcome by misery all over again. One day, returning from the factory, he'd run into Victorine. He hadn't stopped her, he'd simply followed her with his eyes, without moving, wounded by her intact beauty, her confident demeanour. That evening he'd wept for a long time, impervious in his reawakened grief to anything Elisa could do to relieve him. She heard his hard, jerky sobs, saw again his distraught eyes, his agonised face, saw his heart ravaged by a single image. How could it be that so much weakness could live inside his big, rough body?

He remained in a state of total dejection for several days.

One night Elisa woke and leaned over him, scarcely able to make out the shape of his body in the whiteness of the sheets. Time would be needed to cure him, a lot of time. She blamed herself for having celebrated too soon. No doubt he'd rediscover the state of semi-calm he'd known in the preceding weeks, and then perhaps he'd lose it again and fall back into his present misery . . . And so it would go on endlessly, perhaps for months. What if he never got better, if he kept these faraway eyes, this suffering face, to the end? The end of what? Elisa was frightened. She leant her head back on the pillow and brushed her forehead with her hand. It was drenched in sweat. In a strange panic she felt all around her the great, fragile, trembling world. She raised her head a little and opened her eyes wide: night was filling the room, and you couldn't tell whether it was immense, infinite, or tiny, a tight little world surrounding her alone. With all her strength she fought against this dead obscurity, rejected this darkness, summoned up comforting images: a meadow where spring blooms, a country road where workers pass, whistling and singing on a blue day; a window open to a triumphant summer, to life itself.

As if a living breath had passed over her forehead, something gentle softened her body. She felt, intact, a lurking hope in the depths of her being. She went back to sleep, her heart open to the possibility of happiness.

The new crisis of despair that Gilles had just survived was like the last gasp of his grief. He rediscovered the sad calm of the earlier days and, towards the end of the winter, entered into a new phase. It wasn't that he showed more tenderness towards Elisa or that he appeared to be definitely cured of Victorine. He continued to suffer and to complain – but without ever mentioning the young girl's name. It was an anonymous grief that he suffered, as if by habit, without any longer knowing the reason for it.

The winter ended without anything happening to disrupt Elisa's new hope. Sometimes she'd stop in the midst of her work, in mid-movement, and a disturbing sense of happiness would immobilise her. Suddenly transfigured, she would abandon herself for a moment completely to the ecstasy of a victory that she felt to be very close.

18

Gilles sowed the border of mignonettes, and the leaves began to sprout, thick and unattractive in a dull green. Every morning Elisa leaned over the border to check the progress of the swollen buds which hadn't yet flowered: they must open soon, insignificant, almost colourless, but offering their invisible charm in small drifts of scent.

No mignonette had flowered yet.

Gilles, hoe in hand, was taking advantage of the last hours of daylight to clean up a bed of young lettuces. He stood, walked slowly up the path, and sat on the bench against the wall of the house. Elisa had been watching him from the kitchen window. She walked down the brick steps, the baby in her arms.

'See how well he's walking already! You only need to help him a bit with your finger . . . '

He looked at the baby with an absent-minded smile.

The twins, who were tired, sat next to Gilles, one on either side, each leaning on her father's arm. Elisa sat down on one of the brick steps, holding the baby close. The meal was ready, it was a nice evening, they could stay like this for a while.

They didn't speak. Darkness fell slowly; nothing moved

in the warm spring air. From somewhere – the bottom of the meadow or a neighbour's garden – came the sound of a child's voice, a faraway sound, barely perceptible, no disturbance to this strange peace.

A precious moment – let no one think of moving or breathing. Was this an ending, or a fragile beginning? It seemed as though something were going to die or be born.

This is how it happened:

As Elisa was about to put out the night-light, Gilles stopped her. 'Wait a moment,' he said, 'I've got something to tell you.'

She turned to him and waited, elbow on the pillow.

'I met her,' he went on. 'You know, Victorine.'

Elisa was alarmed to hear the name he no longer uttered. Gilles smiled. 'Don't worry . . . '

Scornfully, he added, 'I felt absolutely nothing!'

'Let her try and soften me up now,' he boasted, 'and just see how far she gets!' Even if she came back to him, begged him, threw herself at his feet, she wouldn't get through to him any more than if he were a block of stone.

Elisa was looking straight into his calm, slightly mocking face, her huge eyes full of fear.

'Is it really true, Gilles?'

'If I tell you, you know very well you can believe me.'

Elisa knew. They never talked about it any more and she had seen perfectly well that Gilles was better – which didn't prevent his sudden announcement that the sight of Victorine had left him cold from striking her like an unexpected blow.

He went on talking. Yes, he was sure he no longer loved her. Seeing her today had made him fully realise that; he hardly ever thought about it at all now, and if he'd talked about it again this evening it was simply as a result of the encounter and to put Elisa in the picture about his feelings. What a state he'd got himself into because of this bad girl! What a terrible mistake he'd made, spoiling all the happiness that he used to have when he loved Elisa! Now nothing ever made him sad nor amused him; all he felt was a vast indifference. He had the feeling that from now on he would always be like this, that he'd never again grieve, never again feel any happiness at all. He might be a bit at a loss from time to time, but he wouldn't really suffer from it. Not that he wanted things to be different: life was much easier this way. 'It's as if,' he explained, 'nothing at all was happening around me – as if my body was quite empty.'

Elisa's heart was beating very fast. Slightly out of her mind, she was listening to Gilles without completely grasping the meaning of his words. He stopped speaking. Turning back to his side he got ready to sleep. She let her head fall back on the pillow. Little by little she calmed down, made an effort to return gently to reality. She repeated to herself the phrases that Gilles had used: 'Now everything to do with Victorine means no more to me than if I were a block of stone . . . She can come back, go away, disappear altogether – I couldn't care less.'

She has to stop then, so disturbed is she by the force of her emotions. Gilles is cured . . . the moment she has so longed for has finally arrived! This day is finally over, and tomorrow will be a different day. She is free, she can begin to live again! She is free! Alive!

She trembles, catches her breath. Happiness is so heavy on her wounded heart. In a single thought she gathers up the burden of her past misery and for the first time it seems to be too heavy, her shoulders too weak to bear it. She is tired; she has come at last to the close of her martyrdom, but she is so tired.

At the end of her tether, Elisa manages to smile into the night. She is liberated, Gilles is cured, life could start up again. She is alive! From tomorrow, from tomorrow . . . Tonight, she has only an irresistible need to sleep. She slides softly over to the body next to her, lying there so peacefully, lets her head fall heavily on to the shoulder of her loved one. Sleep, nothing but sleep for days on end . . . just like this, on Gilles' shoulder.

As dawn rose, wavering rays of light shone into the bedroom, lighting up the edges of the window, skimming sadly over Elisa's beautiful, exhausted face. Could any hands be gentle enough to nurse that body, any lips be loving enough to welcome her out of that precious sleep?

Gilles had already been up for a while and was washing himself with noisy splashes of water. Elisa awoke, realised that she was late, and hurriedly prepared breakfast with unfeeling, familiar movements. Her head was still full of the heavy sleep, interrupted too soon.

'See you this evening, Lisa!' He waved at her and pulled the door shut behind him.

When the twins had gone off to school Elisa put little Gilles into the baby-chair and went back up to the bed-room.

She hadn't even had time to do her hair. Now she unplaited it; black and shining, it framed her pale, emaciated face. It was long, thick and heavy, over-whelming her weary head. She thinks about the previous night and her strange feeling of exaltation, feels again the dead sense of happiness. Gilles is cured – so why is there no room for rejoicing? Did he not say that he was no longer in love with Victorine, that nothing she did could affect him any more? Elisa stopped herself at that point. Yes, he had said that, but he had said many other things besides, the full meaning of which still hadn't entirely come across to her but which were already causing her pain. 'It's as if nothing was happening around me . . . '

So her task isn't yet over after all. The image of Victorine has been erased from Gilles' heart but Elisa still has to reoccupy its emptiness: the love they once shared still has to be built all over again.

She leans over to pick up one of her combs, raises her head again too quickly and sees a shimmer of little gold stars in front of her eyes. She sits down, stays still for a moment, hands crossed in her lap, eyes fixed. Gilles . . . the love of Gilles? . . . the love of Elisa? . . . Something has withered in her heart.

She gets up and walks slowly about the room. What does she have to do this morning? Rinse the washing, hang it up in the attic, clean the tiles in the kitchen, scour the copper pans, buy some vegetables – what is the point of all those actions? All around her are only dead things. She passes in front of the mirror, sees her dishevelled hair and absent-mindedly, without even plaiting it, pulls it together into a heavy chignon, barely pinning it up.

She goes downstairs, and her hands begin their pointless travail.

My love – where is my love? Nowhere. You were inside me, you were my whole being. My love? Nothing. I am nothing. Appearances, mirages, hopes, the moving games of the world. Life goes on. Where are you, Elisa? I'm here . . . my hands are plunging into the cold water, they're pulling out a piece of blue calico and wringing it; the heavy, wet washing is piling up in the wicker basket.

Life goes on, but who is Elisa? I do not recognise this woman, I am nothing. Gilles' woman? Oh my love, why have you abandoned me?

Lifting up the full basket she holds it against her hips. The baby is calling for her; turning away, she walks slowly up the stairs.

The attic has been heated by the sun; it smells of warm pinewood. She puts the basket down, makes a ghost of a gesture and lets her arms fall.

She is supposed to take the box filled with wooden clothes-pegs, pull the pieces of washing out of the basket, one by one, and hang them all along the line. And then? Another task to do . . . Why? With what aim in view? For no reason at all – there is no aim. And at the end of the day what will happen? Nothing. And tomorrow? The same as today. No, she cannot possibly hang out all this washing, she just cannot do it. Better to wait, to wait for something to happen. This evening perhaps?

'Hello, Elisa. Hello, Gilles. Is dinner ready? Yes, you can eat. Do you love me, Gilles? No, Elisa. And you, Elisa, do you love me? I don't know, Gilles.'

She is haggard, immobile, as she stands by the tall wicker basket. Her loosely pinned hair falls down into her neck. Don't lose courage, Elisa! Nothing has changed inside you. You have accepted so much without ever hating, without ever punishing, without giving in for a single day. Admit this moment of weakness in yourself, just for today; give your exhausted body a chance to recover its strength. In a few days you'll discover that your love hasn't left you after all, you'll find it again, intact, powerful, immovable. Just wait a few days, a few hours. Perhaps even by this evening, when you see that big muscular body in the corduroy work-clothes in the doorway, you'll get back that feeling of immense tenderness that used to paralyse you, as you stood with both hands on the metal rail of the stove. And perhaps Gilles, shining with rediscovered love, will come up and gently kiss your forehead, as he did on that first day. And even if there are only dead things for you here, you might have the chance to fulfil your need for love and life else-where . . . Courage, Elisa! Life is everywhere. Just wait, don't give up on yourself, just wait! Life is about to be reborn . . .

But Elisa doesn't think, doesn't hear, doesn't see. She feels only this strange void all around her. She can't live without her love – even for a single day.

She moves forward, her arms outstretched, groping along in a dead world in which she can no longer find her place. Through the low window of the attic, in the far distance, the high furnaces are pouring out all their flames, all their smoke. But Elisa does not look out. She raises her hands, grips the window frame, climbs up on to the narrow sill: she is so tall that she has to bend her head a little so as not to touch the beams. For a moment she leans her cheek against the plaster of the wall, her eyes closed, her face serene, smiling almost. The window is open: a light spring breeze steals across the fields and comes to rest on her long skirt, making it ripple softly around her ankles.

Eyes still shut, she will slip her head gently against the plaster sill, then under the window frame. She will lean out a little, and in a slow, impassioned gesture, let go the hands that hold her.

Marthe was in the garden next door. At the sound of the body hitting the ground she turned, let out a long scream. People ran up and leaned over, not daring to touch. Marthe stood, grabbed her son's arm with clenched hands and said, in a horrible voice, 'Run, quick, get Gilles!'

The boy turned to his mother in a daze and murmured, as if he didn't know anything any more: 'Gilles?'

'Yes, of course, Gilles – Elisa's man!' Marthe screamed.

Elisa still breathed. A long shudder seized her broken limbs as Marthe spoke – the last words she was to hear.

Translator's Afterword

This new edition of *La Femme de Gilles* forms part of a welcome twenty-first-century revival of the Belgian writer Madeleine Bourdouxhe (1906–96). Originally recommended to the house of Gallimard by the influential literary talent-spotter Jean Paulhan, editor of *La Nouvelle Revue Française*, *La Femme de Gilles* was widely praised on its publication in Paris in 1937. The distinguished critic Ramon Fernandez found it hard to believe it was a first novel: 'The tone and equilibrium are remarkable,' he wrote, 'and the art of conveying silence . . . is flawlessly achieved.' Bourdouxhe told me, her translator and literary agent, that in the end it was her favourite novel, because it was the one that made her name. 'Every now and again I think about it, and I think – "That's not so bad".'

None of the critics who hailed her then as a rising star could have predicted that the reputation of such a gifted thirty-year-old would abruptly go into decline, her career in the literary mainstream virtually over as soon as it began. When I asked her about this in 1988, during one of our many discussions, Bourdouxhe chuckled and shrugged her shoulders. She was a great believer in fate, and publication was always less important to her than writing which, as for so many women throughout history, often had to be done in stolen moments. Writing remained, however, a vocation rather than a peripheral activity. To the very end of her life she would work through the night, in the modern block to the south of Brussels where she had moved from the arty Sablon quarter to be nearer her daughter and granddaughter. 'I have always had a real need to write,' she told me, 'and I just kept on doing it, even though I couldn't often get to Paris to try and place my work. But I always read the new books as they came out.'

The immediate reason for her disappearance from the limelight was the outbreak of the Second World War in 1939 and the subsequent occupation of Belgium and France. Living in Brussels and working actively for the Resistance, she would have nothing to do with publishing houses, Gallimard among them, that had been taken over by the Germans. It was not easy for her to visit Paris and when she did, it was at some risk to her life. On one occasion, she reminisced, she persuaded 'a decent Nazi' to issue her with a permit by bringing him a personally inscribed copy of *La Femme de Gilles*. On another, when she was smuggling leaflets back from the surrealist artist Paul Éluard, she found herself surrounded in the Paris metro by a cordon of German soldiers. Her eyes met those of the leader: he guessed what she was up to; yet he let her go. This image of violence narrowly averted, of a woman travelling alone through the dark occupied city, is like a scene from one of her own stories: secretive, silent, fraught with danger.

In 1943 a small Brussels imprint, Editions Libris, a firm that she felt to be 'above suspicion', published her Paris novel, *A la recherche de Marie*. Over the years that followed, various stories appeared in magazines in France and Belgium, but it was not until the 1980s, when second-wave feminists started to read her and to acknowledge her literary worth, that Bourdouxhe's work began to re-emerge.

In 1985 *La Femme de Gilles* was reprinted in Belgium by Editions Labor, and in the same year a volume of stories, *Sept Nouvelles*, most of which touch upon life under the Occupation, appeared in Paris in a collection edited by Françoise Collin of Editions Tierce. When the Women's Press, London, asked me to read the stories I was immediately drawn to the author's quiet strength. I recognised a confident female vision that although born of her time and place still spoke with an exciting directness. I began to investigate Bourdouxhe's work with a view to translating her into English but my research proved problematic: not only was there little in print, but the story of her life had gone almost unnoticed by literary historians, even in her own country and in France.

By the time I met her in Brussels in 1988 I had finished translating the stories and read most of her other available work in libraries. I had thought of her as a wartime author, and had assumed that her writing career was long over, so the biggest and most welcome surprise was that she had continued to write; indeed that three of the stories were comparatively recent.

She was a slim, elegant woman with a very deep voice, a throaty chuckle, a penetrating gaze and such a strong respect for life that she refused to use flea-killer on her cats. Though reticent by nature, she was clearly delighted at the prospect of her work appearing in translation ('the English were the first to liberate Brussels'), and after my visits would send me letters in shaky but clear handwriting, elaborating on things we had discussed. The resurgence of interest in her work brought her some gratification but no real surprise; she had always retained a confident sense of her value. She was no longer greatly concerned about widespread recognition, knowing that her main literary engagement must be with her own fictional creations rather than with publishers or even readers. It became a standing joke between us that whenever she finished a story, she would put it 'in a drawer'. The act of writing had, perhaps, become an end in itself.

My edition of the stories eventually included a biographical commentary and the long out-of-print *Sous le Pont Mirabeau*, with its original illustrations by Mig

Quinet; it was published by the Women's Press in 1989 as *A Nail, a Rose*. It was followed by translations of *La Femme de Gilles* (Lime Tree, 1992) and *A la Recherche de Marie* (Bloomsbury, 1997). Publication of the work in English, and information about her life, marked a turning-point in the process of rehabilitation. The English novelist Jonathan Coe described her as 'one of the most remarkable literary discoveries of the past few years' and from 1990 to 2000 the *oeuvre* was translated into many languages. It was particularly popular in Germany – where it achieved bestselling status for Piper Verlag – but in the new century most editions again became hard to find, apart from in France and Belgium, where the work is now available from Actes Sud. We are now witnessing a resurgence of critical acclaim that should surely seal her literary reputation once and for all. The process began in Paris in 2009, when a wide-ranging conference was held at the Centre Wallonie-Bruxelles entirely devoted to her life and work. The book of the proceedings, *Relire Madeleine Bourdouxhe*, is the first comprehensive tribute to the writer's achievements.*

It is greatly to the credit of Simone de Beauvoir that she should have remembered Madeleine Bourdouxhe

---

* *Relire Madeleine Bourdouxhe: Regards croisés sur son œuvre littéraire*, eds. Cécile Kovacshazy et Christiane Solte-Gresser, Bruxelles: Peter Lang, 2011.

when she came to compile *The Second Sex*, published by Gallimard in 1949. De Beauvoir praises her there for her subtle observation of the differences between male and female sexuality. Gilles' behaviour in bed, she claims, is typical of the way in which men seek to 'reduce erotic pleasure to an immanent and separately felt sensation'. The very fact that he asks Elisa whether she enjoyed their love-making 'emphasises the separation, changes the act of love into a mechanical operation directed by the male . . . He really seeks domination much more than fusion and reciprocity . . . he likes to have the woman feel humiliated, possessed, in spite of herself; he always wants to take a little more than she gives.'

When I told Bourdouxhe that I had unearthed this passage about her it sparked off lively memories of the friendship between the two women writers, both philosophy graduates of approximately the same age and writing in the same language. 'I knew about her, of course, and I had already met Sartre: soon after the war he published one of my stories in his magazine *Les Temps Modernes*. But it came as a complete surprise to me to find my name in *The Second Sex*. I bought it just because it was a new book, and because it was about women.'

The next time she was in Paris she sought de Beauvoir out. 'I went to that famous café – what's it called? – the Deux Magots – to introduce myself. After that I'd arrange to meet her and Sartre whenever I was in Paris, in a café or a bistro, and we became friends. We would talk about everything under the sun – books, children, men, politics.' She clearly enjoyed these forays into Parisian literary life. Her daughter Marie, born in 1940, fervently recalls the paralysing boredom of wandering up and down the Boulevard St Germain waiting for her mother to emerge from the Brasserie Lipp. 'I knew every leaf of every tree on that stretch of the Boulevard . . . '

It is worth recalling that when *La Femme de Gilles* was first published in 1937 de Beauvoir was still struggling to become a writer herself. She was about to begin work on her own first novel, *L'Invitée*, eventually published in 1943 and misleadingly translated into English as *She Came to Stay* (1949).

Since both novels deal with a *ménage à trois* – de Beauvoir's is based on Sartre's affair with a young protégée of hers – the link between *L'Invitée* and *La Femme de Gilles* is a compelling one. Set in the sophisticated theatre and café life of Paris, on the face of it de Beauvoir's novel could not be more different – and yet adolescent Xavière, the threatening, capricious 'other', bears many resemblances to Victorine; there is an equally violent climax precipitated by the heroine (in this case Françoise murders Xavière, whose physicality obsesses her just as Victorine's obsesses Elisa); and the central dilemma is again exacerbated by over-dependency on a man. For all her urbanity Françoise realises that her life revolves too completely around Pierre, to the extent that nothing really exists for her until she has told him about it: 'her every thought was with him and for him.' In *The Prime of Life* de Beauvoir mentions that she was particularly proud of the narrative structure of this early work – as in *La Femme de Gilles*, characters other than Françoise are occasionally allowed to tell the story, so that 'no character is the repository of absolute truth'.

In our conversations Bourdouxhe was more forthcoming about de Beauvoir as a person than as a writer: although she admired Sartre, particularly for his refusal of the Nobel Prize, she thought that de Beauvoir's work was written 'too much under his influence'. Philosophising is as natural to Simone de Beauvoir's loquacious intellectuals as is silence to the unsophisticated creations of Madeleine Bourdouxhe.

As a novel *La Femme de Gilles* has many of the elements of classical tragedy. The small cast, the contained setting and the symmetrical structure give it a universal quality that lends a passionate intensity to the unfolding drama. And as in a play by Racine, the dénouement is triggered by an event that takes place at the very beginning of the work, after which characters and even narrator are powerless to affect the outcome. Once Victorine has kissed Gilles, there is no turning back.

These turbulent emotions are set in a framework that

achieves its effect by being at once vague and specific. We know that we are near an industrial city in northern Europe, where furnaces spit out their fumes day and night, where pollution and cold winds make gardening a struggle, where a single small table is used for all the basic functions of domestic life – eating, ironing, reading, playing cards or children's games. This is a small world in which life and love are punctuated by the seasons and the factory shifts. It could be almost anywhere; it is, in fact, Liège, where Madeleine Bourdouxhe spent her early childhood. The city is not named, and she was gratified when her compatriot Georges Simenon wrote to tell her that he had spotted the setting.

'I was brought up in Liège, and that had a profound influence on my work,' she told me. 'It was very, very important to me. In those days, before the First World War, all the principal Belgian factories were in Liège: it was a totally industrial area. As a child I can remember the collieries and looking into the dark faces of the men who worked the mines.

'No one in my own family actually went down a mine, you understand – my father was an engineer, he bought and sold machines. But from a very early age I was interested in factories and the people who worked in them, and when I got a bit older I came to know some of them, through my parents' maid, to whom I was very close.'

The vividness with which she recalls her childhood is a measure of Bourdouxhe's intense preoccupation with overlapping memories, with the layers of consciousness that coalesce to create the female personality. Elisa frequently delves into her childhood or adolescent memory, as if seeking solutions to her dilemma in a cumulative sequence of images: walking across town with her mother; arranging her baby sister's hair; frolicking in the woods with Gilles before their marriage. All these vignettes are recollected with such clarity that they seem to have been permanently stored in her brain; and when they become too painful to bear, she herself is capable of putting a stop to them: 'Elisa herself now called a halt to the march-past of images.' Accumulated memories can provide solace too: 'Gilles holding her breasts as she kissed him was such a familiar pose that it seemed to lock the present into the tenderness of the past.'

Bourdouxhe explained this process of interiorisation in a short statement in *Editions de la Nouvelle Revue Française* in October 1937. 'If you watch Elisa from the outside,' she wrote, 'her struggle is barely perceptible. What I wanted to do was to follow Elisa through her interior life. I created her from a composite of the women I saw around me. I'd see a fleeting look, an expression, a smile, for just a moment – then it would be gone . . . but it emanated from something inside them, something that continued to live inside them, and it was that look that created the women they were.'

Though she firmly resists identification with any single school or movement, it is impossible to consider Bourdouxhe's work in complete isolation, particularly when *La Femme de Gilles* slips so easily into the tradition identified by modern feminist critics: the novel in which a docile exterior conceals an inner self that is tormented, deranged even. But unlike most of the female nineteenth-century writers who have been re-examined in this light, Bourdouxhe chooses heroines from the edges of society for whom their marginality is the very essence of their lives, making a male writer, Thomas Hardy, an inevitable point of reference, and one that was originally perceived by Ramon Fernandez in 1937.

Using a proletarian context gives Hardy and Bour-douxhe the opportunity to describe how experience feels in the making. Tess Durbeyfield and Elisa are both natural, sensuous women, instinctive and unintellectual; they make the ingenuous mistake of depending on tactics to attain the happiness they crave, and are denied. Although they have highly developed interior lives, they do not say much – and when they finally speak, it is too late. Both women are, in a sense, martyrs to the concept of love that they embody. For Elisa the pain is made all the more acute by the absence of a confidante: she is alone with 'the greatest pain she has ever known'. To the outside world Elisa may epitomise the perfect wife and mother but when faced with the burden of Gilles' passion for Victorine (which she eventually has to carry for him as well as for herself) she begins to find such expectations intolerable. In the memorable nocturnal scene when she pursues Gilles to the baker's and beyond, leaving the children alone, she stops to rest in a little arbour, a shadowy mass in the snow. She is all pathos, yet she has not quite lost her fire, and muses plaintively upon her fate. Much as she loves her children, her feelings for them are only an extension of her love for Gilles: he is her man, her whole world, and she has 'a right to fight for him'. She considers the possibility that she's been dealt an unfair hand: why should she have been chosen to find fulfilment in this unique way? Today's reader, whom Elisa sometimes pushes to the limits of tolerance, may well be relieved that at least she asks herself the question.

The unprovided answer is that as Elisa trudges further and further along the road to self-destruction she is following her destiny as 'la femme de Gilles' – a label whose double meaning in French grants it a convenient duality of intention, at once ironical and ambiguous. Elisa has had to be both woman and wife 'of' Gilles, yet after the fateful kiss she is no longer his woman, and his wife in name only. Many titles play with naming in this way: Tess cannot really be said to be 'of the d'Urbevilles' – she is indeed ruined by staking her name to the title – and Emma can no more bear to think of herself as 'Madame Bovary' than 'Hedda Gabler' can fully accept that she has become Mrs Tessman. When I asked her about the title of *La Femme de Gilles* Bourdouxhe made it quite clear that she wanted it to suggest both meanings. 'If "wife" alone had been intended, the word used would have been "*épouse*" . . . '

Lacking a confidante, Elisa has to turn to God, though like Tess she finds it hard to focus on prayer and considers the priest's advice unhelpful. In a highly charged, erotic passage she sits in church, eyes wandering, still intent on life in spite of her grief. Her gaze alights upon the statue of an un-named saint who is young, beautiful and dreamy, apparently in a state of masochistic ecstasy at having been pierced by thirteen arrows. She is strongly attracted to him, physically as well as spiritually: 'his young, pink, plaster throat seemed to swell and throb like a wounded pigeon.' He is, of course, Saint Sebastien, the passive martyr, with whom Elisa's identification is complete.

The magnetism exerted over the reader by Tess and Elisa owes much of its force to the attitude of their creators: in Hardy's case, his adoration of Tess (whom even the cows in the dairy choose in preference to the other milk-maids) is so strong that in the second half of the novel she almost eludes his grasp. The narrative of *La*

Femme de Gilles is also heavy with emotional involvement, yet it is a model of economy, clarity and understatement in which whole scenes and lives are conveyed in a single phrase. This stylistic confidence is announced in the breathtaking rapidity of the opening sequence of events. The mood in the first scene – Elisa's torpor at the thought of Gilles's return, his own anticipation of their love-making, the twin girls and the overall picture of domestic bliss – is profoundly ironical, and it is abruptly shattered by the kiss and Elisa's extraordinary 'insight' into the terror of the unknown, the abyss into which she must ultimately, inevitably, fall.

As realisation dawns upon Elisa – 'Gilles no longer loves me' – irony gives way to a compassion that subsequently informs the entire novella. The author identifies fiercely with the agony of the two main protagonists whilst at the same time acting as a kind of counsellor: warning Gilles against the dangers of masculine desire, comforting Elisa and complimenting her upon her female strength, even expressing their emotions for them when she feels she can do it better than they can. This leads to a narration so strong that the author becomes almost another character – a chorus.

When asked about the unusual device of addressing her characters directly, Bourdouxhe told me that she had no alternative. 'The characters take on a life of their own. After I have created them I no longer have any power over them – I simply do what I am told. Sometimes they refuse to obey me . . . '

If the narrator's voice occasionally threatens to overwhelm the reader, it is never complacent, and Bourdouxhe does not hesitate to shift perspective to achieve an effect, to create a permanent state of elasticity between reader, narrator and characters. Tenses are called into play here, especially when she uses the historic present for extended passages. This device is much more common in French than in English and it represents an important element in her style, bringing a cinematic intensity to crucial sections of the story. She uses the present at those moments when she is creating a sense of inevitability which she wants the reader to experience as it happens, or as it happens for her characters: organic and lyrical at the start of the story (and occasionally later), increasingly bleak and helpless, finally tragic and complete.

Whilst the main viewpoint is, of course, Elisa's, or the narrator speaking for Elisa, it is through Gilles that we experience the initial kiss as well as his final violent assault on Victorine, and the story-telling momentarily moves to Elisa's mother and even a passing stranger, who watches Elisa's heavily pregnant body glide past him into the darkness of the night. Only Victorine, with her crimped hair and her 'disgusting' ways, all sexuality and no heart, is denied a narrative contribution, as she chatters pointlessly away.

In contrast Elisa thrives and suffers in the silence that reverberates throughout *La Femme de Gilles* – a silence shattered only by Gilles' confession, his attack on Victorine and then, at the end, the thud of Elisa's falling body. For her creator, Elisa seems to symbolise a nobility that is deeply disturbing. In her *Editions de la Nouvelle Revue Française* statement she describes the suicide as 'an act of heroism': 'I would have liked to save her, but no appeal from life could have reached her; rescue could only have come from within her. And when she no longer was anything, she no longer wanted to be anything any more: she arrived at her end passionately. Annihilation in love – it's pretty much the story of all women. And when you think of this you experience a strange sensation: the life of women is marked by a moving nobility – but how one would like to relieve them of it!'

The denial of authorial responsibility makes the ending all the more catastrophic, all the harder to take, implying as it does that Elisa's mixture of nobility and masochism has somehow become a significant component of her femaleness. When she climbs the stairs to the attic, ignoring the cries of her baby, Elisa is finally, irrevocably, beyond anyone's grasp. Having lost not only the love of Gilles but, more importantly, her love for him, which she sees as the only justification for her existence, she is in effect already dead, already gazing into the abyss. Not even her creator can pull her back. It's this that makes the story of *La Femme de Gilles* so haunting – inevitable and unbearable at the same time.

FAITH EVANS

May 2014